Of Bullies and Bullfrogs

By

Mark Jordan

For Caitlin, who once said that boys had all the
good stories. And for Kevin who always believed
Thanks to Amy, Andrea, Erin, Laura, Lynn,
and Venus who helped me get this done. Special
thanks to Julia Sirosh, who translated the text
into Ukrainian so more children could enjoy it.

ISBN: 979-8-9854467-0-8

Contents

CHAPTER ONE

Ruled by Unwritten Rules

Do you know how many unwritten rules there are about being the new kid at school? It's a serious question. I know there's one unwritten rule that at least one person must pick on you for being new. And then there's my situation. There's no expiration date on teasing somebody for being different.

"Ash-leen Shannongale, go to my office!" shouted Ms. Quinn.

Oh yeah, and then there's the third rule about always getting in trouble for fighting back.

Even though the principal pronounced my name correctly, which was rare for an adult, it wasn't cause for celebration. I still had to go to her office. Which meant I was in trouble. Again. Sure, I have a weird name. It's spelled Aisling, and hardly anybody pronounces it properly because it's Gaelic. Most people say *Aze-ling*, which I don't mind, but it's not really my name. I just put up with it half the time because it's easier. My mom calls me Ash for short. And if I had a friend, she'd probably call me that too.

So, even though getting sent to the principal's office was totally unfair, I went quietly. It's another unwritten rule that not fitting in means a lot of trips to the principal's office, even if you don't deserve it. In this case, Ms. Quinn even saw the whole thing and knew it was all Brock Sullivan's fault. But I would get nowhere by arguing unless you call detention somewhere. I sighed heavily as I yanked open the door that led into Thornhill School's old white stone building. Why do they make the doors at this school so heavy that a kid can hardly open them? Is that another unwritten rule? I turned and marched straight toward Ms. Quinn's office. Except with my head down. Totally humiliated again.

This was all Brock's fault. He just can't leave me alone. I go out of my way to avoid him, so he goes even further out of his way to tease me. And after he goes too far, I call him a name. And yeah, that's what happened. But it's still his fault.

I quietly opened the door to the administrative office. Thankfully, only Mrs. O'Shea was inside, humming an old Irish tune while she typed on the computer. As I sat down on the bench, I could feel my eyes start to turn golden. I know that's a weird thing to say, but I've always been able to feel it. It felt like when it's too bright outside, and you squint to see. Unfortunately, it's never a good thing when my eyes turn that color. Weird stuff happens. I can't explain it.

"Oh dear," said Mrs. O'Shea as she hit the same key harder and harder. "These computers…"

Oops! Well, at least a trashcan didn't catch on fire. That happened at my last school, but the headmaster there totally deserved it. Most of the time, lights just flicker, sometimes electronics stop working. I don't know how or why, but these accidents and the weird feeling in my eyes definitely seem related.

Suddenly I smelled fresh rain. I pulled a handful of hair across my nose. Nope, my hair still smelled like that vanilla shampoo.

"First time here?" whispered the kid who scooted in next to me. "You're the new girl in fifth grade. Transferred from the private school across town. Pronounce your name, Ash-leen, right?"

"Yeah," I sighed quietly. "Wait… You know how to say my name?"

"Of course," said the boy. "It's Gaelic. So, you must be the Shannongale."

"What? How did you…?" I was baffled. How did he? Who was this kid? "You speak Gaelic?"

"I'm Tom," the boy said, holding out his hand until he realized I wasn't going to shake it. I probably should be more polite, but I really wasn't in the mood. "Tom Sceal," he continued. "It looks like you could use some help." He nodded to the principal's office.

"How can you help me?" I said as I studied the kid. His red hair was even more fiery red than mine. He also had bright green eyes and one of those sneaky smiles. "You're in what grade?"

"And you're in a bit of a predicament." Tom Sceal replied. "I bet you've never been in trouble here before."

"And you have?" I asked.

"I pretty much live here," he said proudly. "Trouble's my middle name."

"That, I believe," I replied.

"Look, whatever she says, just apologize," said the boy. "And don't be defiant. She hates that. Trust me."

"I would never..." I began, then I saw him open my sketchbook. "Hey! What are you doing?" I grabbed for it. But he moved so quickly, I missed.

"These are pretty good," said Tom Sceal, leafing quickly through the pages. "But you can do better."

"How would you...?" I asked in a whisper.

Tom Sceal dipped his hand into the pocket of his hoodie and sprinkled some glitter on my book as he muttered, "Show what she knows, in her head and heart. So we see what shows, as purely her art."

The glitter landed on my sketchbook, sparkled for an instant, then vanished.

"What are you doing?" I grabbed back my book.

"Oh, I always carry some fairy dust for when I get into trouble," he said with a smile. "Thought you could use a bit."

"There's no such thing as fairy dust or magic," I said as I looked at my sketchbook. Okay, I know that's not entirely true. I'm pretty sure there's magic. Magical things always happened around my mom. Somehow, she manages to grow vines around the entrance to her art-show booth overnight. And let's not forget my trashcan fires, although there might be a scientific reason for that. Or bad luck. But still, fairy dust? That's a massive stretch, even in my book.

And my book is where Tom Sceal's fairy dust just disappeared. The leather cover felt warm in my hands. But where had the glitter gone? I looked him up and down. Why do only the strange kids talk to me? Is that the fourth unwritten rule? The bell clattered to life, and the door to the hallway whipped open, snapping my attention to it.

Ms. Quinn marched Brock Sullivan past the bench and straight into her office. She directed him with one hand firmly on the back of his striped polo shirt. His eyes were dark, and his face was beet red. But her eyes might have been darker.

The principal closed her office door so hard that the frosted glass pane shook in its frame. I jumped in my seat.

Mrs. O'Shea looked up, over her half-moon reading glasses, first at the door and then at me. Her grey hair had silver highlights woven throughout, and her glasses were on a chain that usually hung in front of her. She smiled apologetically at me.

"I'll be honest, dear," Mrs. O'Shea said with an Irish lilt. "I didn't expect to see you here. But once I saw Brock Sullivan, I knew why."

"He always picks on me," I sighed, slumping my shoulders in resignation.

"That's what boys like him do," replied Mrs. O'Shea. "They pick on nice girls like you, so you react. Then they try to look like the victim."

"He's really good at it," I replied with a frown.

"Oh, sweetie, he's not just good at it," replied Mrs. O'Shea. "He's one of the best." Mrs. O'Shea turned back to her computer and smiled. "Ahh, there we go," she said as she started typing.

I looked for Tom Sceal, but the boy had escaped. In case he returned, I slid my sketchbook under my legs and then sat on it and my hands.

The clock said it only four minutes later, but it seemed like forever until the door to Ms. Quinn's office opened, and Brock Sullivan shuffled out. He looked humiliated but mostly angry as he walked to the bench.

"Sorry, freak," he said in a grumbling snarl without looking at me.

"Mister Sullivan, I said to apologize sincerely," Ms. Quinn commanded from the doorway.

"Sorry I teased you about your ears," Brock said loud enough to be heard.

"And?" Ms. Quinn said, hands on her hips, tapping her toe.

"And I won't do it again," the boy rolled his eyes as he said it. Yeah, that was a lie. He wouldn't even make it the rest of the day without teasing me. He hadn't stopped in the whole month I'd been there, despite countless trips to the principal's office.

Brock turned and raised his palms as if to see if that was good enough. The principal nodded, so he turned to Mrs. O'Shea and grumbled some more.

"Sorry I called you that name," I replied to his back. I called him a *skelpie-limmer*, even though I wasn't exactly sure what it meant.

"Very good." The principal motioned to her office, "Your turn, Miss Shannongale."

"Yes, ma'am," I said as I turned to pick up my sketchbook. It sparkled one more time, and I squinched up my face in surprise. But when I looked up and saw Ms. Quinn's face, I immediately hung my head in shame and walked into her office.

Inside the office were tons of antique books. Every wall was hidden by bookshelves filled with old, leather-bound spines that stepped up and down in red, brown, yellow, and black. Most had faded gold or black lettering that I couldn't read. The smell of leather and old books was strong in the office, but there was another subtle smell — fresh rain.

"What do you have to say for yourself?" Ms. Quinn said as she closed the door. It didn't rattle in its frame this time. Instead, it gently clicked shut.

"I'm sorry, ma'am," I said. "I... I lost my temper."

"You certainly did," agreed the principal as she sat down in the old oak chair. "Where did you learn such a word?"

I paused, then I decided to lie. "A kid at my old school." I hate lying, but the truth was not likely to make this situation any better. "When she said it, the other kid stopped being bratty."

"I would be astonished if any student used that word," replied Ms. Quinn, raising one eyebrow. "It's an old Scottish word, and while quite accurate for Brock Sullivan, we don't say things like that at Thornhill Primary," replied Ms. Quinn. "Even if they tolerated it at Oakville Academy." She looked over the top of her glasses at me, which I'm pretty sure was the universal sign that an adult knows we're lying.

"Yes, ma'am," I looked at my lap. I was glad that even though she knew I was lying, Ms. Quinn wasn't pushing it.

Part of me sighed quietly in relief; the rest of me hung my head in shame. Lying was worse than calling Brock a name. I could feel that familiar, watery pressure behind my eyes building. I inhaled sharply, hoping to make it go away. It didn't. Even though I was on the verge of crying, I wanted the principal to understand that I was not trying to cause trouble.

"Ma'am, It's not fair. I keep telling him to leave me alone, but he won't stop," I sighed. "And when I told him for the fourth time already today, I'm the one who got in trouble."

"Had you just told him to leave you alone, you wouldn't be in trouble," said Ms. Quinn. "But that's not exactly what you did, is it?"

"No, ma'am." I shrugged and sighed again. "But he doesn't listen otherwise."

"I will have to send a note to your mother," Ms. Quinn scribbled on a pink piece of paper. "Give this to Mrs. O'Shea and return to your class."

"Yes, ma'am," I replied. I put on my bravest face as I sniffed back a tear.

"Crying won't do any good," Ms. Quinn said, handing me the slip. "Now go."

"Yes, ma'am," I replied, taking the note and heading for the door. I stopped, turned back, and said, "I truly am sorry."

"Everybody is when they get caught," said Ms. Quinn, without looking up. "Now, go on."

CHAPTER TWO

It's a Frog Eat Frog World

O kay, another unwritten rule is that you always manage to call attention to yourself every time you want to be invisible. Like when you're late to class. You want to run so you're not so late, but you also don't want to get in trouble for running in the hallway. I was pretty sure that all school hallways were designed to make it impossible to be a ninja. I mean, why did they call my shoes sneakers if every step I took shrieked down the long, almost cold hallways? It didn't just hurt my ears, but it dramatically increased the likelihood that somebody would see me and stop me for being late for class.

The building was more than a hundred years old and had once been a teaching hospital for nurses during and after the first

World War. At least that's what Ms. Quinn said when she gave Mom and me the school tour in February. It always smelled clean but never fresh. I was pretty sure the janitor worked in a dentist's office. You know the smell. Not fun.

After climbing the stairs to the second floor, I swore that Room 222 had moved even further down the hallway. Each step echoed off the lockers and walls. Seriously? Why was it so hard to be totally stealthy like a ninja?

Being the new kid, I hated anything that called attention to me, and yet everything did. Of course, when you're the only kid in school with long red hair, it's like you've got a siren on your head. I swear, some days, it was all anybody saw. Okay, there was also my fair skin and freckles that made me seem pale next to anybody else. At Oakville Academy, one kid said I could hide in front of a whiteboard. If it hadn't hurt so much, I might have laughed. It was a pretty good burn.

If that wasn't bad enough, I had never known my dad. Mom had told me that he died when I was just a baby; however, that sad story didn't seem to matter to the other kids at school. Tiffany Treacle had been kind enough to point out that even the kids whose parents were divorced still knew their dads.

I finally reached Room 222 and paused outside the door. Ugh, I hated this, but I pulled open the door.

Have you ever heard a hush of giggles? That's what broke out when I stepped into the room. Miss Desoto, who was sitting on the front of her desk, paused and looked at me. She had an exotic look, with dark cat-like eyes, incredibly long lashes, and straight mahogany brown hair that brushed against her shoulders as she turned.

"Glad you could join us, Aisling," my teacher said with a warm smile that ended in dimples.

"Sorry, ma'am," I looked down and noticed I was clutching my sketchbook. I guess I was kind of holding it like a shield to cover my heart. I handed Miss Desoto the pink note from the principal. The chorus of "ooohs" quickly returned to giggles and snickers as I tried my best to disappear on the way to my seat.

Just before I got there, Brock stuck out his leg to block my path. Part of me wanted to kick it and cause him some pain. Instead, I just rolled my eyes and stepped over his outstretched leg, which he raised, because he's Brock. I almost tumbled into my chair headfirst. Part of me wished I really had kicked him.

"We're reading about frogs in your biology book," said Miss Desoto. "Page 347."

"Yes, ma'am," I replied as I dug my book out of my backpack. The class smelled of new books, drying poster paint, and flowers. It was so much better than the hallway. As I opened my book, I glanced around the room. I wanted to see if anybody was still laughing at me; fortunately, nobody was. On the walls were examples of the projects everybody had worked on so far this year. None of my projects were on the wall. Sure, I'd only been there one month, but my best grade had been a B so far.

"Miss Desoto?" asked Jenna, one of the very few kids in the class who didn't look down on me. "I still don't understand why bullfrogs are considered an invasive species. Haven't we always had bullfrogs here?"

The girl smiled at me; her white teeth sparkled against her dark-brown face. She was trying to redirect the class's attention off the new girl, which I really appreciated.

Jenna was incredibly athletic. She wore her curly black hair back in a bushy ponytail and almost always wore some soccer gear. Today it was warm-up pants and a matching top from the Women's National Team.

"That is a very good question," Miss Desoto stood up and went to the whiteboard. She picked up a blue marker. "Bullfrogs actually came from the southeast, and they have a ravenous appetite..."

"What does ravenous mean?" Michael asked.

"It means they're always hungry," Miss Desoto replied, still drawing a frog on the whiteboard.

"Like you, Michael," Brock said with a laugh as he kicked Michael's chair.

"Mister Sullivan," Miss Desoto turned to Brock. "Would you like another visit to the principal today?"

"Noooo, ma'am," replied Brock.

"Then let us focus on bullfrogs," the teacher said, turning back to the whiteboard.

"So, are you saying that bullfrogs are just big bullies?" Jenna asked, nodding to Brock, who wrinkled up his nose and raised the right side of his mouth in a sneer at her.

"They certainly disrupt the balance of nature," Miss Desoto replied, obviously missing the reference to Brock. "I guess they are kind of like bullies here because they pick on anything smaller than them."

My sketchbook vibrated lightly on my desk. Who was that boy, Tom Sceal, and what did he put on my sketchbook? If it were just glitter, those silver flecks would be everywhere.

"I heard that frogs were cannibals. Is that true?" Tiffany Treacle said with a grimace. The other girls in her squad began a chorus of "Ewww."

Jenna and I looked at each other and shook our heads. Then Jenna rolled her eyes at Tiffany Treacle's friends, which made me giggle a bit.

"Settle down, class," said Miss Desoto. "Your assignment for the week is to write a five-page report on frogs. You can write about any aspect of frogs, but I do not want to see the first page copied from Wikipedia." She looked at Brock, "Does that register, Mr. Sullivan?"

The class snickered. Michael turned around, pointed at him, and laughed.

"Yes, ma'am," said Brock as he rolled his eyes and kicked Michael's seat.

"You can team up in pairs," said Miss Desoto. "We're going to start with some traditional research in the library with real books. I expect you to each reference at least two printed books in your report."

I took notes on the assignment while the rest of the class argued why searching on computers was better.

"You can also search on computers," said Miss Desoto. "But I want you to read a couple of printed books, too. Understood? Good, because Ms. Clarke is waiting for us in the library, so please don't dawdle. Let's go," she indicated the door as the class gathered notebooks and pens or pencils. "Aisling, could I see you for a moment?"

Tiffany Treacle led the chorus of "Ooohs" as they opened the door to the hall.

"Miss Treacle, do you think there is any chance that we could do this without disturbing every other class?" Miss Desoto said without any hint of a question. She turned to me and said, "Aisling, walk with me."

CHAPTER THREE

Research, the Old-Fashioned Way

I waited for my teacher, fully expecting a lecture on calling Brock names.

"I know it's not easy fitting in here," Miss Desoto whispered as we walked behind the class. "Girls like Tiffany never make it easy. But you would do well to avoid Brock Sullivan. He has not yet learned, or at least doesn't care that there are consequences for his behavior."

"Yes, ma'am," I replied with a nod. Miss Desoto smelled like lavender, which always calmed me down a bit.

"Jenna is a good student, and she's pretty new too," Miss Desoto said. "I think she would like to be your friend. I'm going to ask her to be your partner for this project. She can also help you catch up with what you missed during the first semester."

"Thank you, Miss Desoto," I said with a half-smile.

"Don't worry," smiled Miss Desoto. "You'll do fine. You just need to give it some time, and you'll find your place. School is not about fitting in or being invisible, you know. It's about finding your place."

"Yes, ma'am," I said for about the twentieth time that day. It must have been a new personal record. Even though I agreed with her, I was still rooting for invisible.

"Now, when I said that you could write about anything frog-related, I meant it," added Miss Desoto. "You don't have to turn in a boring biology paper. To be honest, every year, I am forced to read too many almost identical science papers, and I get so tired of the same thing over and over again. I am hoping you will give me something entertaining – maybe even magical."

The teacher's eyes sparkled as she spoke, and I couldn't help but grin. It was as if she knew that I loved fairy tales and magical stories. We reached the library just as Ms. Clarke began her lecture on using the school computers for research and not playing games. The librarian pointed out where the biology books would be and ended with, "Of course, if you have any questions, please ask. I know this library like the back of my hand."

The kids all dashed off to get in line for the four computers. I waited for everybody to clear out and then approached Ms. Clarke.

"What can I do for you, dear?" the librarian said over the top of her glasses. She was slender and had on a light blue blouse and dark grey skirt that fell well below her knees. She was wearing thick shoes that must be comfortable because I rarely saw her sit. Her blond hair hid the silver highlights well, and her smile was warm and inviting.

"I was thinking about writing my paper on frogs and magic," I whispered. "But I have no idea where to begin."

"Oh, I like that idea. Hmmm... I think I can help you," smiled Ms. Clarke. "We've got books on fairy tales over here and books on spells the next row over."

"Spells sound fun," I grinned as I followed Ms. Clarke over to a shelf toward the back corner.

"These two shelves will have your fairy tales — everything from Hans Christian Andersen to the Brothers Grimm, as well as folklore from all over the world. Then, if we go around the corner, here you'll find books on witchcraft and spells."

"Thank you, Ms. Clarke." I scanned the titles and slid out a big, well-worn older book titled, *Witchcraft: A Handbook of Spells and Potions*. It smelled like leather and old paper. Then another title caught my eye. The golden letters *Spellcasting* seemed to sparkle at me, so I took that book too.

I looked around and shrugged. Why sit at a table with kids who would just make fun of me? It was quiet back here, so I sat on the floor in the corner and began to read. The old grey linoleum floor felt cool and smooth. I opened the Witchcraft book and found a section all about frogs. This was going to make my report so much easier.

I took careful notes on how frogs and magic have a long history together. I started to draw the stages of tadpoles and frogs in my sketchbook. I was focused on taking notes and trying to get as much done as possible when I heard Brock's all-too-familiar and irritating chuckle. I groaned inside. It must be another unwritten rule that the teaser must pursue the tease relentlessly.

"Eww, look, it's elf-girl," said Brock as he leaned against the bookshelf. "Are you hiding in the corner, so nobody will see you cry?" Without thinking, I held up the *Spellcasting* book.

"I'm studying how to turn you into our class project," I said without looking up. Where that came from, I have no idea, but it worked. Brock stood up straight and stared at me with wide eyes. In return, I looked up and smirked at him. He backed away down the aisle of books and turned right into one of those wire carousels that held books for younger kids.

The crash of metal and clatter of books echoed through the library as Brock and the carousel went down and sprawled across the floor. A couple of Tiffany Treacle's friends shrieked, but most of the class pointed and laughed.

"Mister Sullivan," said Ms. Clarke, who was standing over the boy and his mess in a flash. "I suppose you will be helping me put these back in the right place?"

"But... she... the..." Brock pointed to where I was sitting. Ms. Clarke looked back at me and saw me taking notes quietly.

"Yes, Aisling is doing what we are supposed to do in the library, quietly reading," Ms. Clarke replied. "Now pick that up and put the books back in it. First-grade readers on the bottom, please."

As Brock stood up the carousel and gathered the books, Jenna poked her head around the corner.

"Whatever you said to him, you have to share," Jenna said, laughing. "That was the most scared and embarrassed I've ever seen him." I smiled up at Jenna and picked up the *Spellcasting* book.

"I told him I was studying how to turn him into our class project," I said with a giggle.

"Excellent!" replied Jenna. "Is there actually a spell to do that?"

"I don't know yet, but the threat worked," I replied.

"Well, now we know what he's afraid of," Jenna said with a laugh. "Too bad Halloween isn't this week."

"Maybe we can still have fun at his expense," I whispered with a grin.

"I'm interested," said Jenna. "Tell me more!"

"To be honest, I just wish we could get him to leave me alone."

"Yeah, that's not going to happen," replied Jenna. "He's pretty stubborn. He picked on me relentlessly until you came along."

"I'm sorry," I said.

"Hey," said Jenna. "Miss Desoto said that she'd like us to work together on this project. Want to?"

"That would be great," I said with a big smile. "It's a lot of work for just one person."

"Any ideas?" Jenna asked.

"Miss Desoto suggested I… I mean, *WE* write a report about magic," I replied, probably with more than a little bit of hope in my voice. She smiled, so I made space next to me.

"That's awesome," replied Jenna as she sat down. "Way more fun than trying to compete with Tiffany Treacle's team science project. What have you got?"

I showed Jenna my notes and sketches.

"You drew these?" Jenna asked.

"Yeah, I… I guess," I replied, realizing what I'd sketched for the first time. How did my drawings suddenly get so good? I hadn't noticed that they were better while I was taking notes.

"They're fantastic!" Jenna said as she smiled at me. "We're going to get an A just for that!" Jenna scooted closer and picked up the other book.

"What do you think about a report about why frogs are thought to be enchanted?" I asked.

"You mean like that fairy tale about the frog prince?" replied Jenna.

"Yeah," I said. "Wasn't he under a witch's spell?"

"Like the one you threatened Brock with," asked Jenna. "This is so awesome! After we finish our report, he'll be terrified of us!"

"People already think I'm a freak," I said with a laugh. "Might as well add witch to it."

"We'll be the Witches of Thornhill," Jenna said. "Actually, that sounds pretty amazing!"

"We'll need to dress the part," I said. "Maybe some witchy clothes with striped socks."

"I've got the clothes, but don't we need a black cat?" added Jenna with a giggle.

"I can work on that one." I said, then added, "I think I've worn down my mom on the kitten idea."

"I like the way you think," said Jenna.

"Do you know a kid named Tom Sceal?" I asked her as I looked at my drawings again.

"Is he in our grade?" Jenna said as she opened the book on Spellcasting.

"No..." I replied and then thought about it. "Honestly, I don't know. He talked in riddles mostly. He could be in the other class."

"I don't remember that name," said Jenna, pausing to think. She tilted her head left, then right. "But I'm kinda new too," she shrugged.

"He seems to know everything about this school," I frowned a bit. "Like he's been here for years."

"Why do you ask?" Jenna looked at me curiously.

"No reason," I lied as I traced the very lifelike drawings in my sketchbook. "Just wondered."

"Oh, this is going to be so much fun to research," Jenna said, showing me a section on *Frogs and Spells* in the book.

"Nothing boring about this research," I laughed.

"But the best part is," Jenna whispered, looking around to make sure nobody else was listening. "We'll scare the living daylights out of Brock!" She leaned into me, and we laughed.

CHAPTER FOUR

The Worst Bus Ride Ever

When the last bell rang, Jenna turned to me as we packed up to go home.

"I'll call you after I talk to my mom," Jenna said. "I hope you can come over so we can work on our project together."

"That sounds fun!" I said as I stuffed books into my bag. I put my backpack on my shoulder and hustled down to the bus stop.

To be honest, I truly hated riding the bus home. There was nobody to talk to, and the absolute best rides involved sitting next to some poor first grader who was also shy. The noise level inside that big yellow tin-can usually left my ears ringing for a good half hour. It always felt like we were packed together like those unbaked biscuits in a cardboard tube -- the ones you push on and the dough explodes out.

Even though I raced to get in line to sit up front, I only managed to grab a window seat in the middle.

As the boys climbed on, they pushed and shoved each other. Michael slapped Brock on the back, giving the bully an excuse to spit out his gum straight into my hair.

"Ewww!" I winced as I tried to brush it out. But the more I brushed, the more it stuck in my hair.

"Serves you right, freak!" Brock laughed and jostled his way to the back. I sighed and looked out the window. I hoped somebody nice or quiet would sit next to me.

"Sit down, boys," the driver called to the boys who were fighting for position.

"Beat it, punk," said Clay, one of the bigger boys, as he pushed Brock away from the back row.

"There's one more seat," he said, pointing to the extra space on the backbench.

"Not for you," Clay said. "Sit with the little kids."

Brock's eyes darkened as he was shoved toward the front of the bus.

"Sit down, now!" the driver insisted as she started the bus.

"Aww, not the elf!" Brock looked around to see if somebody would trade.

"Now!" said the bus driver, closing the door. Brock dropped onto the seat next to me and promptly turned around and knelt on the bench to look at his friends.

"Butts in seats or we don't leave," the driver shouted.

Brock spun around, his eyes dark again, crossed his arms, and elbowed me.

"Make room," he said.

I wanted to elbow him back, but then he'd make a scene, and we'd take even longer to get home. So, I pulled my arms even closer and leaned into the window. I hated being called elf-girl; it was so annoying. But to make matters worse, Brock smelled like he hadn't used soap in a week or two. Never mind shampoo. Plus, he was constantly smacking loudly on something in his mouth. I couldn't wait for the bus to pull up at the corner of Primrose and Rowan so I could escape.

About ten excruciating minutes later (which honestly felt like about fifteen times that), the bus finally pulled up to my stop. I stood to leave, but once again, Brock blocked me with his leg up, foot against the seat in front. Since Miss Desoto wasn't watching, I decided to force my way out. I stepped hard on his other foot and pushed past his leg.

"Ow!" Brock squeaked. Then he squirted his apple juice onto my pants and giggled.

I pursed my lips into a scowl and whipped my bag across Brock's face as I climbed over him. My bag must have caught him as he took a drink because it made him cough. I kinda wished it gave him a black eye. Kicking out, I pulled free from the seat and stumbled toward the front of the bus.

Behind me, Brock and a few boys laughed. I didn't look back, but I knew that Brock had managed to squirt the juice, so it looked like I wet my jeans. I lowered my head, growled, and gritted my teeth. I raced down the stairs and out of the bus without looking up.

The door closed, and the bus coughed into motion before I finally exhaled. I was so frustrated by that troll. I pushed my arms straight down by my side and curled my hands into tight fists. I knew my eyes were changing color as I glared at the bus and growled one more time. The bus stalled at the stop sign, and I realized I might have done that. Well, if it took him longer to get home, that would almost make up for everything he'd done to me.

But I felt bad for the other kids. I would have hated being stuck on the bus for one more minute with him. I looked down and saw my tears start to fall, so I ran across the street. I slipped through the front door and closed it as quietly. I went straight to my bedroom, where I kicked off my shoes, tore off my wet jeans, and yanked my t-shirt over my head. I rummaged in my white dresser and pulled out clean shorts and a t-shirt. I slipped them on, flopped onto the bed, and screamed into my pillow. I even hammered my fists on the mattress just to get it all out.

When I sat up and looked in the mirror, my nose, cheeks, and eyes were all the same dark color of red – about what Mom's paint jars called claret. But that didn't matter. Right now, I hated everything about my new school, except Jenna and Miss Desoto. Basically, I pretty much hated my life. Yeah, I know, I could suddenly draw like my mom, but what if that was temporary? I did also finally have a friend. Well, maybe two if you count Tom Sceal, but there was something weird about that kid. Even by my standards. Still, even though those things were awesome, I wasn't done feeling sorry for myself. Not by a long shot.

I looked around the room my mom painted with a little help from me. Magical creatures were hiding behind leaves, rocks, and trees. The ceiling depicted a sunny day with white, puffy clouds. In the corner where the windows met sat my rosemary bush. When it was warm, the plant filled the room with a smell that made me think of having pizza in the forest. Next to my bed was a stack of books.

I scanned the stack of books, then pulled out a well-worn copy of The Ugly Duckling. I opened it to the first page. All of my frustrations bubbled up one more tear. I ran my finger over the drawing of the little gray baby bird that just didn't fit in with the ducklings. "I can totally relate," I told the picture. Then I turned to the end of the book and traced my finger over the graceful swan gliding across the water.

That's it! I knew precisely where I needed to go at that moment. I wiped the tears onto the back of my hand, climbed out of bed, and put on my shoes. I went to pull my hair back into a ponytail, but then I remembered the gum Brock spat into my hair. I picked up my backpack and slid out my sketchbook and pencil.

I closed my eyes for a minute, took a deep breath, and let it all the way out. I inhaled again and opened the door to my room.

"Ash, are you okay?" Mom called from upstairs.

"Yeah," I said. "I just want to sit by the creek."

"I understand, honey," she replied. "Try not to get your shoes wet."

"I promise," I said as I darted out the back door and halfway across the lawn before anybody could catch me. My family had lived in this house for a couple hundred years. The backyard had that deep green look that you only find in old gardens. There were maybe three in all of Thornhill, Massachusetts. Most of our neighbors updated their yards with patios and stuff, but not us. Our yard probably looked like it did a hundred years ago.

I know I looked like a rabbit being chased by a fox. I had that same mixed sense of freedom and fear. I love my mom, but I also knew I was going to be in trouble soon enough. If I could just postpone the punishment long enough to sink my toes into the stream that ran behind our house, I might be able to endure another lecture.

I slowed down as I approached the leafy privet hedge at the end of the property. Seriously, you can't run full speed through a small opening that makes you turn sideways. At least I can't. I tried once. Never again. Instead, I carefully slipped through a small space in the bushes and avoided scratching my face. There it was – my drawing rock. Even on days like today, when all I wanted was to disappear, my rock was waiting for me. I knew that as soon as I climbed aboard, I'd forget every single worry and concern.

Okay, maybe it was technically more of a boulder than a rock. It was almost as tall as my knees on the creek-side and up to my chest in the back. It was also wider than I could reach across. The front half was flat on the top, so I could carefully set my sketchbook and pencil on it. The back angled up, so I could lean against it when I wanted to veg. At that moment, I wanted to sit on the front edge so I could dangle my toes in the water. That always made me happy. Unless it was freezing.

I took off my shoes and socks carefully. In the old oak tree, a couple of birds sang while the water gurgled on its way. It smelled like heaven to me, a mixture of grass and flowers and flowing water. For as long as I could remember, this was my special place.

The creek had a funny name — Thornhill Burn. Mom explained that in the old country, a burn is a stream or brook, which is how it got its name. Still, burn seemed like a funny name for water. Thornhill Chill would have made much more sense.

But Thornhill Burn was its name, and it wasn't terribly wide by our house. It got wider when it joined with Oak Creek near town. There, a small stone bridge crossed it. It was too big to flow through a pipe under the street. I figured that Jillian, who used to be my babysitter, could probably jump across it here with a good run-up, but it was too far for me. I had tried, and my sneakers took days to dry once I managed to get that gooey mud off them.

What hurt the most was that my mom didn't appreciate the effort, which I considered pretty athletic. She could have at least given me credit for trying to jump that far.

I put my white sneakers and pink socks on the bank, two giant steps away from the edge so they wouldn't fall in. Still too close, knowing my luck. I moved the shoes back another big step. The last thing I needed was Mom upset with me for anything else. Once she got that email from the principal… Nope. I was not going to think about that now.

I put my sketchbook and pencil on the rock, then climbed up on the giant stone. It felt cool, which was nice since it was a pretty warm day for March. From the ledge at the front of the rock, I dangled my bare toes in the creek. I leaned back and imagined that I was in the middle of an enchanted forest, like in one of Mom's paintings. The whole area was suddenly alive with fairies, elves, and unicorns. Well, in my imagination.

A hummingbird flew nearby, circled around me, then darted off down the stream. Across the creek, toads called "craaaaaaaa" at one another. It always sounded like they were annoyed at something. Probably at being a toad. Or maybe it was because kids like Brock were called toads too. Hard to blame the amphibians for that.

The tiny green hummingbird whirred close by again, but then he moved across the creek. Up in the trees, the finches and sparrows chattered and chirped sweetly. It made me smile. A dragonfly hummed by, flying left, then zipping suddenly right.

You can say what you want, but this was a magical place. It didn't matter if nobody else believed me. It always made me feel like everything would be good with the world. All I had to do was sit here with my toes in the water.

Then I remembered everything was not good. Soon Mom would read the email from school, and she would have to help me get the gum out of my hair. At least the gum was evidence of him bullying me. Still, there was no way Mom would let me stay home from school tomorrow so I could sit here. It would probably rain anyway. That was my luck.

"Aisling!" my mom called from the back door. I guessed peaceful time was over. I sat up and began picking up my stuff. "Aisling, where are you?" Mom called again.

CHAPTER FIVE

A Narrow Escape

"What is this?" my mom waved her phone in front of me as I walked into the kitchen. I knew better than to say, "Your phone," so I went with the less obvious truth.

"Brock Sullivan was being a jerk," I replied as I kind of slunk into the bright kitchen.

"It doesn't say that, Ash," my mom said, using my nickname. She turned the phone around to read the note. "It says you called him a…" Mom paused, put her hands to her side, then shook the phone at me. "Where did you learn that word?"

"You said it to that teenager yesterday," To be honest, I felt pretty safe with that defense until I saw the look in my mom's eyes. Okay, time for a new approach. I dropped my head and made a mental note that the things I heard Mom say while driving probably shouldn't be used at school or anywhere near adults.

"At least you didn't use a four-letter word," Mom said with a sigh. "What, exactly, did this Brock do to deserve this?"

"He called me elf-girl for like the nine hundredth time," I crossed my arms. "It's hard enough being the new girl in school. Why do I have pointy ears, mom?"

"Well, everybody is different," Mom said gently. "Some people have blond hair and blue eyes; some have black and brown. Some have cream-colored skin, and some have cocoa."

"Yeah, but I don't look like any other kid in the school. I have red hair, eyes that change color, paper-white skin, and pointy ears," I grumbled. "I look like somebody from Middle Earth."

"I don't think you look at all like a hobbit or an orc," she said, thinking that was a good mom joke.

"But I do look like an elf, don't I?" I said, staying on topic.

"And a lot of people will find that very attractive," Mom replied. "At least you look like my daughter." She pulled back her long, dark, copper-brown hair and showed me her own slightly pointy ears. I studied my mom a bit. She was pretty even when she frowned a bit, which she was starting to do.

"Are we freaks?" I asked.

"Did Brock pick on you again?" she replied.

"Mom, he always picks on me," I replied. "That's hardly news."

"Honey," she paused. "Our family has always been picked on."

"Because of our ears?" I asked.

"We've always been a bit different," Mom said. "It's… well…"

"Mom?"

"I don't really know what to say," she said. "I never knew when to tell you, but I guess… I mean, I kind of knew…"

"Mom?" I looked at her. She looked like something horrible had just happened. "You're starting to freak me out."

"I knew it would come out when we transferred you to this school," she said with a sigh. She looked at me like she was trying to remember me. "I guess it's time you knew the truth."

"The truth about what?" I asked.

"You are a halfling," she blurted out. Then she leaned toward me like she was going to hug me.

"A what-ling?" I said, shaking my head.

"A halfling," she repeated. "You and I are part elf."

"Yeah, right," I said, stopping just short of performing an epic eye roll that might have broken a school record. "There's no such thing."

"Halflings are real, so are elves," Mom said. "It's why you've never met your father."

"You're not serious?" I smirked. I scanned my mom's face for signs that this was a joke. I wouldn't put it past her. But she wasn't cracking a smile. She actually looked a little scared. "How am I part elf? I mean, seriously, Mom! How is that even possible?"

"I fell in love," she said with a shrug. "Shannongale women have always enjoyed a magical connection to the fae realm, and when I met your father... I just couldn't help myself."

"This is insane!" I said, trying to wrap my head around this completely... well, insane... idea. I walked to the far side of the room and turned to look at her.

"For as long as there has been a human realm and a fae realm, there have been Shannongale women." Mom paused. "Thousands of years ago, when the Milesians arrived in the Old Country, the Milesians were ready to fight the Tuatha Dé Danann."

"Milesians? Tuatha Dé-who? What are you talking about, Mom?" I interrupted.

"Let me draw it for you," my mom said, pulling out a piece of paper. I walked back and looked over her shoulder. On the paper, she drew an island. As she drew it, it colored itself green.

"What the...?" This conversation just went from crazy to mind-blowing. Except what people usually do with their hands was happening in my brain.

"The Milesian is the old name for humans," she said as she drew some ancient warships. "And the Tuatha Dé Danann..." she drew some fairies and elves. "Is the original name for the faerie folk." Her drawing of the ship landed on the island, and people jumped out, ready for war. "The humans wanted to fight for the harbors, but most of the fae were artists and farmers. So, our leaders decided to divide the kingdom."

"For real?" I couldn't believe my pointy ears. Or my eyes. I couldn't take my eyes off her drawing as it came to life. If this was true, then the fairy dust that Tom Sceal sprinkled on my... I looked at my sketchbook on the table and wondered. I wanted to ask Mom about him, but I also wanted to learn about my ancestry. I turned and studied Mom's face for any sign that this was all just a story to make me feel better.

"It's true, Ash," replied my mom. "The Tuatha Dé Danann took to the forests, streams, and mounds, while the Milesians took the pastures and harbors." In her drawing, the humans built cities, while the fairies and elves created a white shield and disappeared. "Then the two groups asked for ambassadors to serve as go-betweens, to maintain the connection between the two kingdoms. The Shannongales are one of those families."

"The Shannongales. Like you and me?" I shook my head. This made less sense than Tom Sceal dropping glitter in my sketchbook and calling it fairy dust.

"Yes, exactly. You and me," Mom replied. "And your grandmother, and her grandmother, and her grandmother before that."

"And my dad?"

"No, your dad is a pure-blooded elf," said Mom. "But, because he was a military leader, he was forbidden to visit us about ten years ago."

"Wait! Wait! He's still alive?" I asked, even though other phrases ran through my head. "You told me he died in a car crash."

"I told everybody that so they wouldn't ask questions," my mom said. "It wasn't an easy thing to tell you. I just didn't think the truth would make any sense."

"It still doesn't," I said, shaking my head.

"I know this is a lot to take in, Ash," said her mother. "And we can talk a lot more. But there are still consequences for getting into trouble at school."

"Wait, what?" My mom lied to me for ten years, and she got off scot-free because I called Brock a name that she had called somebody else? On the scale of totally not fair, this is way up there. Like way ahead of not having a smartphone and needing to ride the bus to school. I looked at my mom again. No matter what I said, this was not a fight I was going to win. Which is also totally unfair. Just saying.

"You broke the rules at school," she said.

"And you lied to me my whole life!" I shouted.

"I was protecting you," she said.

"But..." I didn't know what to say. I mean, seriously. I just found out that I'm a halfling and my dad's alive, and I'm the one facing consequences? So not fair.

"But how did you do that?" I asked, pointing to the picture. My mom's phone buzzed.

"Just a second, honey." Mom held up her index finger. She put her smartphone to her ear and said, "This is Sarah Shannongale...

Why yes. Oh, that would be... well, let me check." She put her palm over her phone and turned to me. "Jenna Healy's mom says you are working on a project together?"

"Yeah, our frog project for Miss Desoto." I nodded. Perfect timing. There's no way I should be punished for calling Brock a skelpie-limmer right after finding out my whole life has been a lie!

"She asked if you could come over and work on it with Jenna," replied Mom in a whisper.

"Mom, we really need to," I said, pretending it was inconvenient. "It's due on Monday."

"Yes, that would be perfect. Okay, let me get your address," my mom said into the phone. She tore a scrap of paper from her drawing and quickly wrote 18 Primrose on it. "Oh, that's just a mile down the road. We'll be there shortly." She hung up the phone and looked at me.

"Well, I guess I won't be grounding you," my mom said. "Go get a scrunchy for your hair and whatever you need for your report. We're going to the Healy's house."

"Um, Mom," I said, pointing to my head. "Brock spit gum into my hair. Can you help me?"

"Alright, let's get that out first," she replied. She led me to the kitchen counter, where she found a jar of coconut butter. Slowly, she began to massage the white goo into my hair. The smell of coconut relaxed my fists that I didn't realize I'd been making this whole time.

"You were teasing about that halfling stuff, right?" I asked.

"No, it's real," replied my mom. "I just didn't know how to tell you. I was trying to protect you, and I guess I screwed up." She focused on the knot as the pink gum began to slide out of my hair. "You are part elf."

"So, I guess I can't get mad when Brock calls me elf-girl anymore?"

My mom's frown cracked into a smile. "You know, that might stop it," she said after she worked the gum free. She hugged me. "If you act like it's a compliment, maybe he'll stop. If Brock can't get the response he wants from you, he'll try to get it somewhere else."

"I'll try, Mom," I said, wrinkling the corners of my eyes.

"I know it's hard," my mom offered.

"In the library, I kind of got him back," I said, trying (and failing) at hiding my devious smile.

"How did you do that?" Mom said, looking at me a little sideways.

"I told him I was looking for spells to turn him into a frog," I giggled.

"Oh, that's a good one!" her mom smiled. "I just hope your…"

"My what?" I replied.

"I just hope your teacher didn't hear that too," my mom replied. But I'm pretty sure that's not what she was going to say.

CHAPTER SIX

Making Friends and Escaping Consequences

"Thanks for inviting me over," I whispered as we sat at the Healy's kitchen counter. "I was about to get grounded for calling Brock a *skelpie-limmer*."

"I wondered what you called him?" Jenna said with a laugh. "Now, I have to look up what that means." She turned to the laptop next to her and typed in the word.

"I probably should have looked it up before I called him that," I replied.

"It says that a *skelpie-limmer* is a badly behaved child, deserving of punishment," said Jenna.

"So, it does fit!" I replied. "Like Ms. Quinn said."

"Where'd you learn it?" Jenna asked. "It says it's an old word that's obsolete."

I nodded toward my mom and then bowed my head. "My mom yelled it at a teenager yesterday."

"I learn most of my bad words from my brothers," said Jenna. "And they get me into *sooo* much trouble."

"I can only imagine," I replied. "Some days, I'm glad I'm an only kid."

"It's a dream for me," said Jenna. "So why did you change clothes?"

"You should have seen what Brock did on the bus," I shook my head. "It was the worst ride of my life."

"I had a feeling he was going to get back at you," said Jenna. "He's just mean."

"He really is," I said. I looked up at our moms sitting on the sofa. "Hey, do our moms know each other?"

"My mom said that they met at the art fair," Jenna replied. "My parents bought one of your mom's paintings. It's no wonder your drawings are great."

"Thanks!" I said, looking at my friend, then down. I'm glad she hadn't seen my drawings before they got good today. I looked up and asked, "Did you find the fairies hiding in the painting?"

"What? No!" said Jenna with a big smile.

"Yeah, she sneaks a magical creature into each painting," I answered. "I have spent hours trying to find them."

"That is so cool," said Jenna. "I wonder what my dad will think of that?"

"Why?" I asked.

"He's a doctor, so it's all science with him," replied Jenna. "No magic."

"Doctors do like science to explain everything," I said, nodding. "Speaking of magic, why does it smell so good here?"

"Oh! My mom made us cookies," said Jenna with a big smile. "Want one?" Jenna jumped up and dashed over to the stove. The kitchen was lined with cherry cabinets and marble counters. It was kind of like our kitchen because it had a skylight and an island, but the room wasn't as bright. It felt more elegant.

"You bet!" I said as I sat up in my seat.

"They're still warm," said Jenna. "But I think that makes them even yummier." Jenna carried over a plate of cookies. She set it down between them and grinned, "Help yourself!"

"Mmm, so good," I practically moaned as I took a bite. There is something about melty chocolate that makes the whole world seem awesome. "Are you still okay with doing frogs and magic for our project?"

"I really like that idea," replied Jenna with a mouthful of cookie. "Plus, my mom told me that if the teacher ever drops a hint about what we should do, do that. It's the easiest way to get a good grade."

"I could totally use an A right now," I said as I pulled my library books from my backpack. "This school is a lot harder than Oakville Academy."

"Really?" Jenna busted out a laugh. "They always talk as though we're the uneducated ones."

"We have a lot more homework here," I said. "It always felt like Oakville was just daycare for older kids."

"Why did you go there?" asked Jenna.

"My mom taught art there," I replied. "So, I got to go for free. But she quit when I transferred to Thornhill."

Yeah, I might have left off the part about starring as elf-girl in Victoria's TikTok video.

"I wish I could take art classes from your mom," said Jenna. "So, does this mean you're not some richie-rich kid?"

"Not even close!" I replied. "I have to ride the bus to our school! Rich kids don't ride buses."

"Enough said," Jenna said with a chuckle.

I opened the book to where I'd left a bookmark. "Check this out. When I was reading this book on witches, I found that originally, witches were considered good. They were the healers. But when people began to think that witches were evil, frogs and toads also became signs of bad things."

"Really," Jenna said as she took notes. "I wonder if it's because frogs can live in the water and on land?"

"That's it!" I said, nodding as I sketched a frog in a pond. "People must have thought it was magic."

"We can write about that!" Jenna said.

As Jenna and I looked through our library books, our moms sipped tea in the living room. I glanced up, met my mother's eyes, and smiled. Then I went back to searching for answers to Jenna's questions while Jenna took notes.

"Did you find any spells for turning somebody into a frog?" Jenna asked.

"Like Brock?" I asked.

"It would solve a lot of problems," Jenna replied.

"Let's see!"

For the next hour, we went over every page of the spell and witchcraft books we had brought home from the library, searching for a way to turn somebody into a frog or a toad.

"Rats," Jenna said, leaning back in her chair. "I thought for sure we'd find something."

"Me too," I sighed. "I guess that was wishful thinking."

"What is wishful thinking?" my mom asked as she put her hand on my shoulder.

"We thought there might be a spell or potion to turn Brock into a frog," said Jenna with a resigned smirk. "But we found nothing."

"Ah, but sometimes the best magic is what we create in a person's mind," my mom leaned in and almost whispered. "Tell Brock that you found the spell, and you're just waiting for the right time. Like Thursday's full moon."

"But we don't have a spell," I replied, honestly.

"No, but he doesn't know that," replied Mom. "And he'll spend all day worried that maybe during the full moon, he will become a frog."

"That's mean," I said with a giggle.

"I love it!" Jenna exclaimed. "He might even try to be nice."

"I'd be happy if he left us alone," I added.

"Girls, I hate to break up this magical study fest, but Aisling and I need to go," my mom said.

"Awww," we said in unison. But I knew better than to push it. I already got out of one punishment, so I put my books back into my backpack. I went to grab my sketchbook, but Mom picked it up instead.

"Ash, these are superb," said Mom.

"I know," agreed Jenna. "We're going to get an A for sure!"

Mom kept looking at my drawings, running her finger over the lines.

"Mom?" I looked at my mother, a little concerned. What was she doing?

"Sorry, it's just…" Mom closed the book and handed it to me. Then she smiled warmly at Jenna and her mom. "Thank you for having us over. Tomorrow, why don't you come to our house?"

"That would be lovely," said Mrs. Healy as she put her hand on Jenna.

"Thanks for the cookies," I added. "They were delicious."

"How many cookies did you have?" mom asked.

"Not enough," Jenna said with a smile.

CHAPTER SEVEN

Dinner and Aftermath

We rode home in silence, which is not normal. Usually, we talk. Often because it's the only time I feel safe to do so all day. Yeah, I kinda suck at talking at school because I forget things and get embarrassed. Plus, I'd much rather stay invisible. My mom kept trying to say something, but each time she stopped. I knew something was bothering her, but I didn't want to bring it up just in case it reminded her of the consequences I might have escaped.

As for me, my head was racing around the idea that if I actually was an elf, maybe it's possible that Tom Sceal did enchant my sketchbook. And if he did that, and it wasn't my artistic skill drawing these things, would it go away? What if my new talent was like a twenty-four-hour bug?

When we finally got home, Mom made my favorite mac and cheese for dinner. She never did the whole out-of-a-box thing, though. I loved how she cooked it with real cheese, which always tasted way better than the orange powder in the store-bought kind. Plus, the smell of the different cheeses melting together made my mouth water.

As we ate in silence. I had approximately two thousand, seven hundred, and sixty-three questions racing through my mind, most of them multi-part questions. And I was pretty sure Mom had a bunch too. Gah! The silence was killing me. I had to do something. If I didn't, this unspoken stuff would make it hard to focus on anything. Like sleep or even my other homework.

"Mom?" I asked, putting down my fork. "You were teasing about me being an elf, right?"

"Oh," she said, coming back to the moment. "No, not... no. Actually, I was just thinking. I was about your age when I found out, too."

"How did you feel?" I asked.

"Probably the same as you," she replied. "Confused, overwhelmed."

"And my dad?" I said, looking down.

"Ash, I feel awful about that," she replied. "There's a war between the dark and light fae. It's been going on for almost ten years, and it's too dangerous for him to come here."

"Do you miss him?" I asked.

"More than I can explain," said my mom, smiling through a pair of very wet eyes. "And I know you've had to grow up without a father, just like I did. Unfortunately, that's pretty common for Shannongale women. It's one reason why we never take our husband's last name."

"Does he miss us?" I asked, kind of hopefully.

"Oh honey, he misses us so much every day," she said, reaching across the table and squeezing my hand. "He sends me messages all the time to see how you're doing."

"How?" I said, looking at her phone with my best confused look, which was an honestly confused look because I was truly... what's another word for confused? Perplexed!

"You'll laugh," she replied. "A little house finch comes and sings to me each morning."

"You understand the birds?" I shook my head in disbelief. "How is that...?"

"You will probably learn how pretty soon," she replied. My mom understands birds. Great! Now we've gone from totally unbelievable to straight out of a Disney movie.

"But he does care?" was what I asked after pondering another three hundred and twenty-one new questions.

Mom nodded. Then she took a breath. "A lot of stuff has happened today. I was thinking about your drawings. How they suddenly..."

"You mean how my drawings finally look like what I imagine in my head?" I finished.

"Yes, but it was so sudden…" She put down her fork and looked at me. "Your drawings were pretty good before. It's like you just unlocked your talent. Did anything happen?"

"I don't know," I shrugged. "I was in the library, taking notes on frogs and magic, and everything I drew looked just like I imagined it would. They didn't look like little kid drawings anymore." Okay, maybe Tom Sceal's fairy dust helped, but my mom, the artist, was proud of my drawings, and I guess I wanted all of that praise for myself. I mean, who wouldn't?

"They're amazing, honey," Mom said with a gentle smile. "Soon, you'll be ready to have your own booth at the art fair."

"Thanks, Mom, but my dream is to share a booth with you," I said, mainly because it was true.

"I think we can do that this summer," she replied.

"What did you think of the Healys?" I asked, hoping the adults got along so life would be easier for us kids.

"I really like them," Mom said with a smile.

"Yeah, Jenna is pretty much the nicest girl in school," I said. "She's the only one who doesn't judge me or pick on me."

"Do you think that's because she's different, too?" she asked.

"Maybe," I said, shrugging. "I guess we're both outcasts, even though we're kind of exact opposites."

"Her mom was telling me that Jenna had a hard time fitting in at the school, too," said Mom. "Do other kids pick on her?"

"Only Brock," I said. "The others leave her alone. Maybe that's because she spends most of recess out on the field, making the boys look bad at soccer."

"And what do you do?" Mom cocked her head to the left.

"I sit and draw," I said. "It calms me down."

"I know how that feels," she nodded. She thought for a second. "You know, if you're doing your paper on frogs and magic, you should look on that old bookshelf. That's where all of your grandmothers' books are."

"Oh, cool!" Wow! I had never really examined that shelf. When I was a little kid, I wasn't allowed to touch them. As I grew up, I was terrified that I'd get in trouble if I read one. But now I had permission! I rushed over to the rows of old books, almost tripping over my backpack on the way. I just wanted to get to them before Mom changed her mind. I was just about to grab a book called *"Familiars and Magickal Pets"* when my finger touched a large, leather-bound book with faded golden letters on the spine.

The title, which had been a series of lines and slashes, rearranged itself to read *"Spells and Spellcasting."* The title lit up when I touched the book. This will sound weird, but I swear I heard somebody whisper the word *"Magic,"* so I looked around. Mom was the only one there, and she was still cleaning the dishes about ten giant steps away. I shook my head and pulled down the oversized book. It was heavier than I thought.

I set it on the wooden coffee table and opened it to the first tan-colored page. The book didn't look like any of the books in the library. It was full of drawings and handwritten notes like it was somebody's diary or notebook. The pictures were of mortars and pestles, herbs, flowers, and dried plants. There were tons of several different spells, all of them poems like the one Tom Sceal had said when he dropped the glitter onto my sketchbook.

No. That couldn't be why. I mean, seriously, what a strange boy. What guy carries glitter in his hoodie pocket?

"Ash, I think it's time for bed," Mom called from the kitchen table. Man, I must have been reading for two hours. How was that possible? I didn't even notice that Mom had finished cleaning the kitchen and sat back down at the kitchen table.

"Okay," I replied, a little confused. "I think I'm going to read a little bit in bed."

"Sounds good," Mom said as she looked at her phone. "I'll come and tuck you in shortly."

I hauled the ancient book into bed with me. The book fell open to a page with a cool drawing of a shield and a short poem or spell on it, but it was in a strange language.

"Did the Ogham reveal itself to you?" asked my mom as she read over my shoulder.

"What's Ogham?" I replied, totally confused.

"The marks on the cover," she answered. "The book is written in Ogham, an old language. It only translates when magic is awake in you."

"Seriously?" How freaky was this going to get? An ancient book that translates itself? Seriously?

"It's how we protect ourselves from people who would call us witches," said Mom. None of this was making sense to me, but I was so tired.

"I guess you're looking to protect yourself?" said my mom as she studied the shield. "Or do we need to protect somebody else?"

"I just want Brock to leave Jenna and me alone," I replied. Now my eyes felt really heavy.

"Well," Mom said as she gently closed the book. She leaned in and kissed me on the head. "Let's see what we can conjure up tomorrow."

CHAPTER EIGHT

Odder and Odder

Halfway through class the next morning, I could have sworn that I saw the clock tick backward twice, maybe three times. I mean, school always drags on, but to have time go in reverse is just not fair! As we went over the math questions from last night, I focused on paying attention (since nothing else I've tried over the past five years has worked). To my surprise and delight, I got all of the answers correct.

"Very good, class," said Miss Desoto as she collected the homework. "Tonight, I want you to use your homework time to work on your reports. That way, you won't have to rush to finish them over the weekend."

Jenna looked at me and smiled. I was so happy that my mom and Mrs. Healy had worked out how Jenna could come home with me, even if it meant we both had to ride the bus. It was nice having a friend, especially one like Jenna. We seemed to have the same sense of justice and humor, just with very different styles.

Take our clothes. Today Jenna was wearing long blue shorts, a white soccer team uniform from Paris with the Eifel Tower in the circle over her heart. Over the jersey, she had a blue warm-up jacket from the same team and black indoor soccer shoes (I know because I asked her). Meanwhile, I was wearing jeans, a pink t-shirt with a gold heart, a white sweatshirt, and white ballet slipper-sneakers. My shoes looked like canvas ballet slippers on top, with a stretchy band across the middle of my foot. They were like gym shoes on the bottoms, making them much more practical than real ballet slippers.

Most importantly to me, they were both cute and comfortable. Not that anybody noticed, but I did. Unfortunately, they were highly impractical for sports. The last time I tried to kick a ball with them, my shoe went twice as high and about twenty paces further than the ball.

I jumped a bit when the bell rang. Loud noises do that to me, even when they're welcome breaks. Although, if I was perfectly honest, I only liked recess because it was a break from classes. But it was also when I was most likely to be harassed by the Brocks and Tiffanies of the world. After spending time in the principal's office yesterday, pretty much the last thing I wanted was to have Brock get me in trouble for the second day in a row.

As the kids all raced outside, I knew that Jenna would head out to the soccer field. After all, the girl kept a ball at her feet during class. It didn't bother me. I just hoped to sit in a corner outside and doodle without getting teased for a change. I found a picnic table in the sun. For some reason, it had been dragged away from the rows of tables where everybody ate lunch on nice days. But I didn't care how it got there. I just liked that it was in the corner, with the hedge behind me so nobody could sneak up. I sat down, opened my sketchbook, drew four dots, and started connecting them with lines.

My mom taught me how to do these Zen doodles as a way to relax when I was at Oakville Academy. I drew a box around the dots and then started filling in the middle with a series of arcs and swirls connecting the dots. As I drew, one of the curves became a braided cord, and then the rope curled back on itself, tying a loose knot. Part of the fun of these doodles was not trying to draw anything, just letting the pencil go where it wanted and seeing what happened. As I sketched, I could feel the tension in my forearms and hands relax. I even wiggled my toes within my shoes.

I looked up at the mostly overcast sky because it smelled like it was about to rain.

"That's cool," Tom Sceal slid in beside me.

"Eep!" I jumped. "Where did you come from?" This boy had a disturbing tendency of appearing out of thin air.

"There," he said, using his thumb to point to the school building over his shoulder. "I like your doodles. But why do you need to relax?"

"Only one person likes me here," I said. "And how did you know...?"

"I like you," Tom said with his signature, toothy grin.

"Thanks," I replied, blushing a bit but also totally scared by that thought. "I guess I just want to relax before I have to go back to class with Brock Sullivan."

"He's a bully," Tom nodded.

"Totally," I agreed.

"You know I can help with him," said Tom Sceal.

"How?" I said, not convinced. "Do you have a big brother?"

"Size isn't the only thing that boy is afraid of," Tom Sceal said with a smirk.

"He is afraid of being turned into a frog," I replied.

"That's a good one," replied Tom. "But you know, most bullies are more terrified of being exposed."

"Exposed?" Aisling squinted, trying to make sense of this conversation.

"Yes," replied Tom Sceal. He leaned in and whispered. "Most bullies are afraid that people will find out that they're not as strong or as smart or as confident as they want you to think they are."

"That's so true!" I agreed as I brushed my hair back. One hair got caught in my fingers, so I wiggled them, and a single strand of red hair fell onto my sketchbook.

"They pick on others to make themselves look better," Tom smiled. "Now, pay close attention." He took my stray red hair and held it above my sketchbook. He twirled the hair in the air and then placed it carefully back into the sketchbook. He focused on it, closed the book, and whispered. *"What you draw will be, until the sun meets the sea. Just draw with intent, then add your breath, to see the possibility."* He opened his eyes and smiled at me. I gave him my best what-the-what look.

"What were you doing?" I asked. "Was that a limerick?"

"It came from that part of the world," he said with a mischievous grin. "I was just helping you with your bully, of course."

"How will that help?" I asked.

"Did you not hear?" Tom Sceal replied. "I thought I was as clear as a bell."

"Oh, you were clear," I said as I shook my head. "But I think your bell is clearly cracked. Did you cast a spell on my sketchbook?"

"A spell?" Tom Sceal looked a bit hurt. "I don't do spells."

"So, what?" I looked at him closely. "Was it a charm? An enchantment?"

"Why would I waste a perfectly good charm on a sketchbook?" Tom shrugged his shoulders and shook his head as if that made zero sense.

"What class are you in?" I asked him, shaking my head at this strange kid.

"None right now," Tom said. "It's recess."

"You know what I mean," I said.

"Oh, that one," Tom Sceal pointed to a window overlooking the playground.

"Up there?" I said as I tried to follow his finger. There was a whole floor of classrooms above mine, some for science, one for special education, three for advanced studies.

When I looked back, Tom Sceal had vanished just as fast as he appeared. I looked around but couldn't see my hair anywhere. I looked at my sketchbook, but there was no sign there either. Was this like the fairy dust?

CHAPTER NINE

Can't Catch a Break

"Ugh, it's elf girl!" shouted Brock.

"Can't you just leave me alone?" I said, standing up and slamming my sketchbook closed. "Is that too much to ask?" I stormed off before he could get any closer or say anything else. I mean, seriously, is it too much to ask to be left alone? Can't he pretend I don't exist, like Tiffany does? To some, that might seem sad, but to me, that would be a blessing! I walked to the door to go inside since he'd never wait by the door to be let in. I leaned against the wall and slid down the cool white stone until I was seated with my knees up. I put my sketchbook on my thighs and began to draw. The more I sketched, the more I relaxed.

Of course, as soon as I relaxed, that's when the bell directly overhead erupted. I slammed my sketchbook closed while jumping to my feet. Had anybody seen, they would have thought I was a gymnast. I looked down and shook my head. Now I understood when Spider-Man said his senses were tingling. My whole body was alive and tingling. I could feel the tag on my t-shirt, the thickness of my jeans, and the band that kept my shoes on my feet. I wondered if that spell or enchantment or whatever Tom Sceal had done was causing this. It couldn't be him. That was just nonsense. But where was the hair? And the fairy dust?

Then again, I was part elf. And that title did change when I looked at it. Who knew what else was possible?

I looked around but couldn't spot him in the throng of kids rushing in from the playground. Why me? Does he know I'm part elf? Was he pranking me? All this thinking and wondering was giving me a headache.

"Hey!" Jenna said as she grabbed my hand. "Come on, let's see if Miss Desoto will give us time to work on our project."

"Great!" I beamed at my only friend. Well, technically, I guess Tom Sceal might be considered a friendly-ish person. After all, girls with one friend can't be too picky about their second friend.

Unfortunately, Miss Desoto was not swayed by Jenna's pleas nor my puppy eyes, which almost always work. Finally, the teacher conceded that if everybody behaved and focused, we could use the last hour of the day to work on their projects. We returned to our seats as the rest of the class stumbled in. My sketchbook almost vibrated like a smartphone being called. I looked at it and wondered.

"Are you two trying to be the teacher's pet?" Brock whispered as he plopped down in his seat. Jenna rolled her eyes and turned three fingers up to form a W and then to the side to make an E as she mouthed the word *Whatever*. I fought back a laugh, smiled at Jenna, then shook my head at Brock. Fortunately, history class went by quickly. Tiffany used up a great deal of it to explain that she had watched Hamilton, which is a musical for adults (at least that's what my mom said). I can't imagine being smart enough to help write the constitution and then develop the entire country's financial plan.

When the bell finally rang for lunch, Brock turned and said, "Let's get away from these freaks. Elf girl's ugly face is making me lose my appetite."

"Ignore him," Jenna said, which made me smile a bit. I knew it was a tired smile. I was so exhausted by his constant picking on me and name-calling that his stupid insults didn't even hurt anymore. "Let's go eat," Jenna added with a smile.

I had to admit, being friends with Jenna made school easier. The weather was overcast and raining, so we ate inside the cafeteria. It was noisy — the kid-to-adult ratio was probably a hundred to one — plus, the noise was bouncing off the walls inside the cafeteria.

We sat at the edge of a long table away from the cool kids so we could talk quietly.

"Tom Sceal sat beside me again," I told Jenna as we unpacked our lunch bags.

"I swear I've never heard of him. Is he in our grade?" Jenna said just before taking a bite of her sandwich.

"No..." I replied and then thought about it. "I don't know. He never gives me an answer. He could be in the other class."

"I've never heard that name," said Jenna, pausing to think. She tilted her head left, then right. "But I'm kinda new too," she shrugged.

"He keeps talking in rhymes," I frowned a bit. "Like he's doing magic."

"Like pulling a rabbit out of a hat?" Jenna asked.

"No," I frowned a bit. "Like spells and enchantments."

"Seriously?" Jenna studied me. "Like the kind we're researching for our report?"

"Yeah," I said. "First, he sprinkled some glitter over my sketchbook and said I could draw better," I was thinking through what I said. It was like I was solving a puzzle in my head.

"Draw better than you already do?" Jenna said. "Geeze, does he think you're Leonardo da Vinci?"

"But that's the thing," I replied. "My drawings did get better. What you saw was after he sprinkled the dust."

"Seriously? Do you have any of that dust left?" Jenna asked with a smile. "I want to sprinkle some on my feet!"

"I wish!" I answered with a laugh. I could recall the whole scene on the bench perfectly. "I thought there would be glitter everywhere, but there was none."

"Yeah, that stuff usually shows up for weeks," Jenna agreed. "For Halloween, I went as a soccer fairy, and the glitter from my wings and wand kept showing up on my stuff through Christmas."

"I know, right?" I replied. "Look."

I showed my sketchbook to Jenna. Nothing sparkled or glittered, but I noticed a new thin red thread in the binding. I ran my finger over the stitching. "Wait. See this red thread? It wasn't here before."

"Are you sure?" Jenna looked at the sketchbook closely. The red ribbon seemed to be woven into the brown stitching on the spine of my sketchbook.

"Positive," I said. "This sketchbook is… well, special to me. My mom gave it to me when I transferred here. It's the only thing that stops me from screaming every day."

"I get that," said Jenna. "Soccer does that for me. If I couldn't run around and kick something at least once a day, I'd go crazy."

I smiled at Jenna. Even though we looked like exact opposites, we were also very much alike. I opened the sketchbook to the first page of notes about frogs and took a bite of my sandwich. Tomato and cheese. Sometimes Mom knew the exact right thing to make for me. I was particularly happy Mom made me lunch because it must have been burrito day at the cafeteria. The smell of overcooked cumin and tomato sauce overwhelmed everything else.

"See, these are fantastic," Jenna said with a smile.

"Yeah, but look at the page earlier," I turned back. The drawings were shaky and much simpler. "That was what I was drawing when I called Brock that name."

"Whoa," said Jenna. "These are pretty good, but the ones on the next page are like your mom's," she said while flipping the page back and forth.

"I didn't notice until you pointed it out at the library," I told her. "And then during the first recess today, that kid, Tom Sceal, took one of my hairs, twirled it, and said a spell or something..."

"And now you have a red thread in the cover of your book," finished Jenna. "This is so cool. We're studying frogs and witches and spells, and magical stuff is happening to you!"

"It's kinda freaky, don't you think?" I took the sketchbook back and closed it, then picked up my sandwich. "Sometimes, I wonder if I'm imagining all of it."

"Well, I don't think you are," said Jenna firmly. "Let's find this Tom Sceal. Do you see him anywhere?"

We scanned the tables while we ate.

"He has flaming red hair," I said. "And today, he's wearing a blue striped shirt with a green hoodie," I added, thinking back to earlier this morning.

Both of us stood up to look. Tom Sceal's bright red hair should have stood out in the sea of blonds and brunettes, but he was not there. We looked at each other and shrugged. I frowned as we sat back down.

"It seems he only shows up when I'm alone," I groaned. "Or maybe I'm going crazy."

"Or maybe Mrs. O'Shea knows," Jenna suggested. "Let's go ask her."

We walked into the school's office. I paused by the bench, looking from it to the office with the glass pane door, but Jenna pulled me toward the counter.

"Hi girls, what can I help you with?" Mrs. O'Shea smiled at us. "Oh, are you here about the note for the bus?" She handed Jenna a note.

"Hi, Mrs. O'Shea, thanks!" Jenna said. "Actually, we were wondering about a kid who goes to school here."

"Oh," the school secretary said as she clicked the mouse and typed a few letters into the computer. The sleek black machine looked completely out of place in the musty office with ancient and very sturdy golden oak furniture. "What is his or her name?"

"Tom Sceal," I said.

Mrs. O'Shea stopped typing and looked at us.

"You... talked to... Tom Sceal?" she asked.

"I did," I said, turning to indicate the bench. "He was sitting here next to me yesterday, just before Ms. Quinn came in with Brock Sullivan."

"I don't think that's possible, Luv," said Mrs. O'Shea gently. She tapped her finger to her lips. "But, then again, you are a Shannongale."

"I'm sorry, but what do you mean?" I leaned forward. "That's my last name, but…"

"Oh, I'm sorry, Luv," said Mrs. O'Shea. "Nobody told you about your family?"

"What should they have told me?" I asked. I looked at Jenna, who just shrugged.

"Well, it's not for me to say," Mrs. O'Shea leaned in. "But strange things always happen when a Shannongale girl goes to school here."

"My mom went to school here?" I said, wide-eyed.

"Oh yes, and your grandmother, and I'm pretty sure there was one before that too," Mrs. O'Shea replied, almost counting on her fingers. "At least, they were all here when the different troubles started."

"The troubles?" I interrupted.

"You should ask your mum about that," Mrs. O'Shea said.

"Wait, but who is Tom Sceal?" Jenna asked.

"He's the one who starts the troubles," said Mrs. O'Shea. "Well, with your mum, anyway. You'd do well to stay far away from him."

"How is that even possible?" I asked. "He's a kid, and my mom…"

"Best ask your mum," Mrs. O'Shea said. "Jenna, don't forget to show that note to the driver so you can take the bus with Aisling. Now run along, you two. The bell's going to ring."

"But...?" I stammered again.

"Run along. You can't be late again," said Mrs. O'Shea with a shooing motion.

CHAPTER TEN

Just Be Quiet

Okay, I had a really hard time concentrating on science after that conversation with Mrs. O'Shea. What did she mean? What troubles? Who or what is Tom Sceal? What about my mom? And what kind of history does my family have at this school? With all these thoughts racing around my brain, you can't blame me for forgetting to focus. So, I might have been staring out the window, trying to solve the puzzle of Tom Sceal and magic rather than listening to the teacher.

"Aisling?" Miss Desoto said. "I doubt the answer is out there."

Brock laughed a little too loud. He turned and sneered, "Why don't you draw something nice today, like me!" Then he turned back around, laughing still.

"Brock Sullivan, you do realize that you are just one misstep shy of another detention," Miss Desoto said sternly. "I would strongly suggest that you leave your classmates alone unless you want to spend another late afternoon with Mr. Findlay."

According to what Jenna's brothers had told her, Mr. Findlay ran detention like a chore detail. The kids had to pick up trash around the playground and cafeteria and then help the janitor. Neither of us had ever been in detention. Still, I was afraid that I had gotten into enough trouble so far this week that I might also be on the edge of spending my first afternoon picking up trash.

However, even the threat of detention wasn't enough to stop Brock from pestering me. He waited until Miss Desoto started to write The Ecosystem of Thornhill on the whiteboard, then he turned around and made a face at me.

I ignored it and continued taking notes when a spitball hit my forehead and landed on my page. As gross as it was, I had to deal with it, so I flicked it off, and it hit Brock in the face.

"Hey!" he chirped.

"Brock Sullivan, turn around," Miss Desoto said. "Right now."

"But..."

"No buts, turn around or go to the principal's office."

Brock grumbled about it not being fair as he turned around. I grabbed my little bottle of hand sanitizer and put a dab on my fingers and smeared it all over my fingers and forehead, then wiped it with a tissue. You can never be too safe when it comes to Brock and germs.

The problem was that I knew my eyes were turning gold again. I tried to slow my breathing to relax, but it was not helping.

Part of me wanted his pants to catch on fire, but I knew that was wrong. Then I remembered how frightened he was when I said I was looking for a spell.

Maybe I could have some fun with him.

I quietly tore a page of paper from my sketchbook and placed it under my notes from class. On the torn page, I began quickly drawing Brock while still paying attention to Miss Desoto. I sketched his square head, his ears that stuck out almost sideways, his pug nose, and the freckles that splattered across his nose. Each time he turned around to mock me, I took a mental picture and then filled in a bit of detail on his face. I drew his arms and shirt. All in all, it was a good likeness of him.

Then I drew a piece of tape over his mouth.

I had to be cautious, though. I continued to take notes and to pay attention as I sketched the bully. The last thing I wanted or needed was to get caught because I was lost in thought while drawing a picture of Brock. I would never live that down.

I even raised my hand to explain why the creek was called Thornhill Burn, which made Miss Desoto smile. Of course, that's when Brock turned around and made a face. I just gave him my best "like I care" look. It seemed to work because Brock stopped and turned around quickly. I smiled at Jenna because she had taught me that look when we were working on our report yesterday.

At recess, the rain cleared up. I pocketed the drawing in my jeans so I could use it to scare Brock, just in case he wouldn't leave me alone.

As it was, Brock behaved as he usually did. He started calling us names, and when that didn't work, he threw a four-square ball at us as we were standing and talking. It bounced perfectly for Jenna, who kicked it right back at Brock. The red ball hit him hard in the stomach before he could react, knocking the wind out of him. It was pretty funny, and we giggled as he rolled around on the wet ground. We both knew he was exaggerating the pain in an attempt to try to get us in trouble. But it backfired.

Brock didn't realize until it was too late that four of the older boys saw it. They started teasing Brock, whose face was now red from both the blow and the embarrassment. When Brock finally got his breath back, he stumbled into the boys' bathroom to escape. I have to admit, I completely forgot about the drawing, and the rest of the school day went by uneventfully.

The note allowed Jenna to join me for the bus ride home. I hoped that Mom could have picked us up, but Jenna said she wanted to ride the bus. We raced to the bus and grabbed the first available bench, four rows from the front. I knew better than to sit toward the back, but I still wondered how the little kids always got in front of me.

"It's the ugly squad," Brock said as he walked by us. "Ugly and smelly," he finished as he sat on the bench behind and across from us. I was on the aisle and not happy about it. Jenna was much better at getting him to shut up.

"If anybody smells, it's you," said Jenna. "Are you allergic to soap?"

"Shaddup!" replied Brock. "At least I'm…"

"At least you… what? Got hurt by a ball kicked by a girl?" Jenna asked, and all the boys started laughing, except Brock.

"Who says you're a girl?" Brock replied. "You're both freaks."

As I squirmed in my seat, I felt something poke my hip. I slipped my hand into my pocket to see what it was and remembered the drawing. Smiling, I pulled out the piece of paper and carefully unfolded it.

"You want to see something freaky?" I whispered as I showed the sketch to Jenna, who laughed.

"Let me see that!" Brock said as he snatched the drawing away. His eyes got wide when he saw it. "Who drew this?"

"I did," I said proudly. "And we put a spell on it."

"Baloney!" Brock said as he swallowed hard. It was easy to see that he wasn't as sure as he pretended to be.

"Ha!" Michael took the drawing from Brock. "That looks just like you! With tape over your mouth!"

"Does not!" Brock pulled back.

"All we have to do is blow on it, and the spell is complete," I said, crossing my arms confidently. "And you'll magically shut up."

"Do it!" Michael exclaimed, grabbing the page from Brock. "Please! I want to see Brock shut up."

"If Brock shuts up, how much will you pay us?" asked Jenna. The boys all laughed and fished for coins in their pockets.

"I've got a quarter," Michael said.

"We've got fifty cents back here," Clay, one of the older boys, laughed.

"I dare you," said Brock, his eyes narrowing in anger.

"Go on," Jenna whispered. "Just to see his face when you do."

They had called my bluff. Oh well, if it didn't work, it still took Brock down a notch. So I took a deep breath and blew as the bus jerked to a standstill.

"Come on, girls, this is your stop," the bus driver called out. We grabbed our bags, hurried down the aisle, and jumped off the bus while everybody else laughed.

CHAPTER ELEVEN

The Troubles

"Hi, Mom! We're home," I shouted as we hurried into the big, white farmhouse-style home. I closed the dark green door and led Jenna through the entryway to the kitchen. The farmhouse was older than the school, but it had been updated. The kitchen was bright, with light reflecting off the white cabinets and seasoned oak countertop.

"Be right down, sweetie," my mom called from upstairs.

"Seriously, did you see his face?" Jenna whispered. "I thought he was going to cry."

"Are you sure you want me to ask her about the troubles?" I whispered to Jenna, who looked back at me and nodded.

"I want to know, too," Jenna said in a hushed voice. "This is the most exciting thing to happen at Thornhill since I started."

We set our bags next to each other on the small round table. The table and matching Windsor chairs had white legs and wooden tops. A vase full of fresh flowers dominated the table, and the windows were open so they could hear the birds singing.

"Okay, that might have been the best prank ever," Jenna said, laughing.

"It was pretty funny to watch him back up," I giggled. "I think he's afraid of me now."

"Oh, for sure," said Jenna quietly. "But how are you going to ask your mom about you-know-who?"

"Not sure," I replied. "I'm kind of afraid of the answer."

"Why?" asked Jenna quietly.

"Because I'm afraid that Tom Sceal's magic will go away," I replied.

"Tom Sceal?" Mom said as she rounded the corner. "Where did you hear that name?"

"He, umm, sat next to me on the bench," I answered. "Why? Who is he?"

"Oh dear," Mom sat down. Actually, she more collapsed onto the chair. "He's back."

"Ms. Shannongale," Jenna said gently. "We asked Mrs. O'Shea about him. She said you would know."

"Oh dear," repeated Mom. "Oh dear, oh dear, oh dear."

"Mom?" I put my arm on her shoulder. "Are you okay?"

"Just give me a second," Mom stood and retrieved a half-full glass of water from the counter.

I motioned with my head, and Jenna smiled. I got the water pitcher from the fridge and poured glasses for both of us while my mother recovered from… well, to be honest, I wasn't sure what Mom was recovering from.

"Oh, forgive my manners," Mom said as she noticed me putting the glasses on the table. "Hello Jenna, thank you for coming over to work with Aisling. It's nice to see you."

"Thank you, Ms. Shannongale," smiled Jenna.

"Mom, what's so bad about Tom Sceal?" I asked. "Nobody wants to say anything about him."

"I thought we were done with him," she replied.

"Mom?" I waited until my mom looked at me before continuing. "Who is Tom Sceal?"

"Tom Sceal is a troublemaker," replied Mom. "He lives to make trouble for people."

"He's like Brock?" asked Jenna.

"Much worse," said Mom. "But… I thought he was bound."

"Bound?" Jenna asked. "What does that mean?

"And what is he?" I asked. "He looks like a boy…"

"Oh, he's no boy," replied Mom. "He's an imp. A full-on, devious imp."

"An imp?" asked Jenna, squinting in concentration as she tried to understand the conversation.

"Like a for-real version of all the stories you read me?" I asked.

"What's an imp?" asked Jenna again.

"Sorry, Jenna. I forgot that you haven't heard all of the bedtime stories I've told Aisling. Let's see. You both know what fairies and elves are?" Mom said. We both nodded. "Well, an imp is a mischievous elf or fairy." My mom got up and went to the bookshelf. She pulled down a large, leather-bound book and leafed through it. "I'm only showing this to you because you're Aisling's best friend and ally."

We smiled at each other, then looked at the book

"There," said Mom pointing to a picture that looked just like Tom Sceal.

"That's him, alright," I said. "But he's… real…"

"Aren't magical beings just a myth?" asked Jenna, twirling her hair unconsciously as she watched my mom.

"Unfortunately, he's very real," said Mom. "I wish he were just a myth because an imp can cause a lot of trouble. Somebody must have unbound him."

"Unbound him?" I looked at Jenna, who had no answers either. Nothing Mom said made any more sense than what Mrs. O'Shea said.

"Somebody must have cast a spell or traded a dream," Mom said, as she looked far off like she was watching a movie play in her head.

"You can trade dreams?" Jenna asked.

"Mom, none of this is making sense!" I shouted. How can I piece together this puzzle with only a quarter of the pieces?

"Things rarely do when Tom Sceal is around," replied Mom. She finished her glass of water and looked around for something else to drink.

"Aisling, tell your mom about the enchantment," prodded Jenna, nodding to my mom.

"Oh no, please tell me he did not..." Mom threw her head back. "What was it this time?"

"He sat next to me twice," I said. "And both times, he said a little poem with my sketchbook."

"He put an enchantment on your sketchbook?" Mom asked. She opened her hand, indicating that she wanted to see the sketchbook.

"Well, the first time, he said that my drawings were good but that I could do much better," I said as I pulled my sketchbook from my backpack. "And then he sprinkled some glitter in my notebook. But when the glitter landed, it disappeared."

"There's no sign of glitter," said Jenna. "We looked closely because I wanted some for my soccer shoes."

"That's when I started to draw better," I said. "Even you noticed."

"Oh, honey, you've always had an eye for art," said Mom. "But the change was quite dramatic. Hmmm," she paused. "He must have removed your *constaic*."

"My what?" Now my mom was actually speaking a foreign language.

"Your *constaic* – he removed the block that was preventing your skill from coming through," explained my mom.

"You mean I always had this skill, but it was blocked?" I replied. "Why?"

"It was for your own good," mom said. "Otherwise, you would have attracted more attention too soon."

"Mom, I'm just a kid who wants to draw," I said. "Nobody ever pays any attention to me."

"This means that your drawing ability is the good deed," my mom said thoughtfully. "So, what could be the contrary?"

"The contrary?" asked Jenna.

"Every bit of magic that an imp does has a good and contrary side," replied Mom. "Aisling's drawings are what she always wanted them to be, and that's good. But what's the contrary?"

"You mean the bad?" I asked.

"Not necessarily bad, just contrary to what somebody wants," answered Mom. "You see, imps like Tom Sceal usually show up to teach somebody a lesson. The hard way."

"What happened to you?" I asked, sitting down.

"Well," Mom said, then paused to think and compose herself. "Like you, I wanted to draw better. Tom Sceal appeared, and suddenly I could draw the way I wanted to. Just like it worked for you. However, we didn't have a Brock in our class. Instead, there was a girl, Linda Everhart, who thought she was better than everybody else."

"That's Tiffany Treacle," Jenna and I said in unison.

"Linda must have made somebody furious," mom continued. "Because Tom Sceal was sent to teach her a lesson."

"How?" I asked, leaning in.

"Well, Tom Sceal knew she was relentless in picking on me, so he gave me the power to have anything I draw come true…"

"What you draw will be, until the sun meets the sea…" I recited without thinking.

"Yes!" said mom, and then just as quickly. "Oh no!"

"Is that the spell he used on you, too?" said Jenna.

"You have to be very careful what you draw, Aisling," she said. "What were the last three lines?"

"Just draw with intent, and then add your breath, to see the possibility," I continued. No idea why I remembered that, but I did.

"Whatever you do," said mom. "Don't blow on your drawings."

"Uh oh," I stood up. I'm pretty sure everybody could see how scared I was.

"The bus?" said Jenna.

"The bus," I nodded.

"What happened on the bus?" Mom leaned forward, looking at the two of us.

"I drew a picture of Brock with some tape over his mouth," I said.

"We thought it would be fun to scare him," said Jenna. "So, we told him that we had cast a spell on it, and all we had to do was blow on it."

"Did you?" Mom looked at me. I swallowed hard. "Did you blow on the drawing?" my mother asked again.

"All the kids were cheering her on," said Jenna, looking back and forth between the two of us.

"Did you blow?" My mom insisted as she studied me carefully.

"I did," I finally said, bowing my head.

"And what happened?" Mom asked firmly.

"I don't know," I said with a sniff. "It was our stop." I looked to Jenna for support, and Jenna nodded in agreement.

"Do you think...?" Jenna started to ask.

"We'll find out tomorrow, I guess," replied mom as she sat back.

"How?" we said together while leaning in.

"Well, if all the kids saw it, they'll either call you a witch," mom said, putting her face into her hands. "Or they'll tease you for not being one."

CHAPTER TWELVE

An Unlikely Defense

As you can imagine, we had a pretty tough time concentrating on our report. I know I had at least three thousand questions, and Jenna probably had almost as many. You can understand why we kept asking my mom about every story that came up in our reading.

"Is it possible to turn somebody into a frog," Jenna asked.

"And if somebody did, would a kiss break the spell?" I added.

"Unfortunately, it is," said mom. "Which is why you have to be very careful, Ash."

"Could Aisling draw our homework being done?" Jenna asked.

"That is absolutely forbidden," mom replied. "You will never learn if you use magic for things like that."

"But what if…" I started to ask, but my mom knew I was headed into what-if territory.

"Girls," mom said. "I know you probably have a thousand questions, and the answer is always going to be, *what do you know in your heart to be the right thing?*" We nodded, so my mom continued, "I do have one request for you both. Please do not tell anybody about this. It could cause a lot of problems for all three of us."

"We promise," we said.

After Jenna's mom picked her up, I didn't know what to think. Yesterday I learned I was part elf. Today I have magical powers. What could happen tomorrow?

As you might imagine, I pretty much just rolled around in bed for a couple of hours before I finally crawled into bed with mom. Not sure any of us got sleep, but we both were still until the pre-dawn light slipped into the room. We didn't talk; we just held hands.

As we were getting ready, both of us with rings under our eyes, I finally turned to mom and asked, "Could you please drive me to school today? I don't want to ride the bus. You know, just in case."

"Of course, honey," she smiled. "I need to talk to Mrs. O'Shea anyway."

"You do?" I looked up from packing my lunch in mid-yawn. "Am I going to be in trouble again?"

"I hope not, honey," she said. "But Mrs. O'Shea knows what Tom Sceal can do. She needs to be prepared, just in case."

"Just in case what?" I looked at my mom with wide eyes. I was pretty much wide awake now. Even more awake than mom, who had just finished her coffee.

"Just in case things get out of hand," mom said. "I don't want you taking the blame for Tom Sceal's shenanigans."

"Shenanigans?" I looked at mom.

"That's what they call the trouble an imp causes," she said. "When I was your age, I had to change schools because of it." Mom paused. "And I am not making you go back to the Academy. I will home-school you before I let that happen."

As much as I was afraid, I smiled. At least mom understood how bad Oakville Academy was for me. We drove to the school in silence and arrived before the bus. While mom went to the administration office, I scurried to Miss Desoto's classroom. I wanted to put off any taunting for as long as I could.

Why did I do that yesterday on the bus? It was like I was somebody else for a minute – somebody like Jenna, who never took any grief from Brock. At that moment, I was definitely not the girl who tried to be invisible most of the time. I reached Room 222, opened the door tentatively, and saw Miss Desoto at her desk.

"Hello, Aisling, you're early," said the teacher. She was wearing black slacks and a cornflower-blue top that was untucked. The blue contrasted beautifully with her golden-brown wrists and neck. Her smile stretched across her heart-shaped face.

"Hi, Miss Desoto," I said, playing with the collar on my heather-grey top. "Can I sit in here? I promise to be quiet."

"Sure," Miss Desoto smiled. "Is everything okay?"

"Yeah... no..." I shook my head as I sat down and pulled out my books.

"What's wrong," the teacher stood and walked over to my desk.

"I told Brock Sullivan that I put a spell on him," I said. "And all the kids on the bus heard it."

"I see," said Miss Desoto. "Now you're afraid they'll tease you?"

"Yes," I couldn't make eye contact with my teacher.

"Did the threat get him to leave you alone?" Miss Desoto asked with a smile.

"I guess," I said.

"Well, if they tease you, just say that you knew it would get him to shut up," Miss Desoto reached forward and brushed my hair out of my face. She tucked it behind my ear and noticed how pointed they were. "You didn't really put a spell on him, did you?"

"No," I replied, quickly covering my ears. I could feel my cheeks burn. "But Tom Sceal..."

"Why do I know that name?" Miss Desoto said. She squinted and looked up and to the right. "Oh, Mrs. O'Shea and Ms. Quinn were talking about him yesterday."

The bell rang. The noise in the hallway grew louder by the second as kids rushed to their classrooms. Lockers rattled open and banged shut.

"We'll talk a bit later, okay?" Miss Desoto said with a smile. I tightened my lips and smiled at my teacher as the other kids burst into the room.

They rushed in until they saw me. Then everybody slowed down, and a couple even backed up. The class formed a wide circle around me until Brock Sullivan burst through.

"You're a witch!" he shouted, pointing his finger at her.

"Brock Sullivan, that is no way to talk," Miss Desoto stood up. "Now, please take your seats."

"I guess it worked," Jenna whispered as she sat next to me.

"I guess so," I sighed. "What now?"

Jenna shrugged, and I prepared for the worst. I figured home-schooling with my mom wouldn't be bad. At least I'd get a lot of art classes that way.

"Exactly what happened?" Miss Desoto asked. Of course, everybody talked at once, which didn't answer the teacher's question at all. She raised her hands like a conductor, then made the sign to end the noise.

"Brock Sullivan, since you were, once again, at the center of this controversy, tell me what happened."

"Elf-girl put a spell on me, and it made me lose my voice," said Brock.

"And yet, here you are, calling her names in a very clear voice," replied our teacher.

"Well," Brock stammered. "My voice came back."

"Of course, it did," said Miss Desoto, coming around to lean against the front of her desk.

"I saw it," said Michael. "It was great! Kept him quiet the rest of the bus ride home." He fished in his pocket, pulled out three quarters, and handed them to Jenna. "We'll pay you more if you do it again."

The class erupted into giggles, which compelled a red-faced Brock to kick Michael's chair. Miss Desoto gave the kids a chance to laugh before she spoke.

"Believe me, Brock Sullivan, if I could pay Aisling seventy-five cents to keep you quiet all day, I would," Miss Desoto said. "But that wouldn't solve the problem, would it?" The teacher walked over to where Brock sat. "Mr. Sullivan, I've seen you do a lot of things to get under people's skin, but this is quite imaginative, even for you. Now apologize to Aisling for calling her a witch."

"No way!" Brock crossed his arms. "She is a witch."

"Miss Desoto," Tiffany Treacle spoke up with her sickly-sweet smile. "Perhaps we could test Aisling to see if she is a witch?" She watched as Miss Desoto returned to the front of the class, and then Tiffany's smile turned into an evil sneer as the girl turned to look at me.

"And how would you do that?" said Miss Desoto, wheeling around fast enough to catch the sneer. "Look, there are a lot of things we can't explain. Brock losing his voice on the bus could be the power of suggestion. Or a trick that he played as another way to torment the new girl."

She stood, crossed her arms, and paced the width of the classroom before moving back behind her desk. She put her hands on the desktop and leaned forward. "Know this. I will not tolerate name-calling in my class." Miss Desoto narrowed her eyes as she looked from Brock to Tiffany. "Name-calling is a form of bullying, just as much as punching or kicking somebody smaller than you. And any form of bullying will get you detention in this classroom and at this school. Repeat offenders will be expelled. Is that understood?"

The class nodded and murmured in agreement. Jenna looked at me, so I shrugged. I'm pretty sure we were both wondering what in the heck had just happened. We had gone from being witches to being victims in seconds.

"Now, everybody, pull out your math books and turn to page forty-three," said Miss Desoto.

As the class got out their books, pencils, and paper, Brock turned around and glared at me. He held up a scrawled note that read, "This isn't over yet!"

CHAPTER THIRTEEN

A Frog in His Throat

When the bell rang for recess, I did not move quickly to leave. To be honest, I wanted to stay safe, and staying behind in class felt about as safe as anywhere at school. I was reasonably and fairly concerned about what Brock might do.

"You okay?" Jenna whispered.

"Yeah," I lied.

"I've got a game with the older boys," said Jenna. "I want to kick their butts."

"I bet you win," I replied. Jenna smiled one more time, then turned and dashed off.

"Come on, Aisling," said Miss Desoto. "I need a break too."

"Yes, ma'am," I said.

I gathered my sketchbook and pencil and decided the library would be pretty safe. There's no way Brock would go there on recess. I slipped into the library unseen and quickly darted to my favorite corner of the library, back by the volumes on witchcraft and spells. I pulled down an old book of spells and drew a picture of women in gowns dancing around a fire.

I erased a couple of lines and was about to blow away the erasing until I remembered the enchantment. The last thing I needed now was a bonfire in the library. I imagined trying to explain that to Ms. Clarke and the principal. There was nothing good that could come from that.

Instead, I swept the page clean with the back of my hand and kept on drawing. Not blowing on my drawings was going to be difficult. When the bell rang, I put the book on the cart for Ms. Clarke and walked back to class, feeling less uneasy. Drawing always helped.

"Out of my way, freak!" Brock shoved me in the back, and I fell to my hands and knees. My sketchbook skittered across the floor. Brock laughed over his shoulder as he ran on toward class.

"You okay?" Jenna said, offering a hand to help me up.

"Why is he so awful?" I asked, fighting back a tear.

"Because he's a jerk," said Jenna as I gathered up my sketchbook. "I guess he's always been this way. Even his brothers can't stand him."

"Maybe that's why?" I wondered. "Can you imagine being called a jerk and getting into trouble all of the time? Even at home?"

"He seems to like it," said Jenna. "Last year, he set the record for days in detention."

"No wonder Tom Sceal…" I started but then stopped.

"Yeah," said Jenna. "But who sent Tom Sceal?"

"Maybe if we figure that out, we can get them to stop things before I accidentally do something horrible," I said as I sniffed at a tear. I summoned what was left of my courage and walked into class just as the second bell rang.

"Did you get a boo-boo, freak?" Brock said under his breath as I passed him.

"Do you really want to mess with her?" Jenna hissed. Then she put her finger and thumb together and motioned across her face like she was zipping her mouth shut.

"There! You admit it!" Brock shouted.

"Admit what?" said Miss Desoto, looking up.

"She admitted they put a curse on me to make me lose my voice," said Brock.

"Well, obviously, it didn't work," said Miss Desoto. "Now, if we're done trying to re-enact the Salem Witch Trials of 1693, perhaps we can turn to our history books. Today, we'll be studying the Navajo tribe. Can anybody tell me what part of the world the Navajo call home?"

I raised my hand this time. Miss Desoto smiled and nodded at me. "Aisling?"

"Their reservations are in Northern Arizona and New Mexico, and Southern Utah and Colorado," I answered.

"Very good," said Miss Desoto. "Now, what are the Navajo most famous for?"

The discussion was lively. The class talked about kachina dolls, blankets, pottery, and their homes. Before we knew it, the lunch bell rang. Even I wasn't dawdling this time. The tables had turned, and nobody believed Brock now, but he was scared.

Jenna forgot her lunch and went to get something from the cafeteria while I saved us a spot in the sun. Mom had packed me some hot mac-and-cheese in a thermos, plus some fruit and a brownie. As I unpacked my lunch, I paused to inhale the smell of mom's cooking. I looked at my dessert and decided to share it with Jenna, so I left the brownie in my bag. Instead, I pulled out the apple juice carton. Satisfied, I waited for Jenna and then looked up because it smelled like fresh rain again.

"She'll be a minute," said Tom Sceal sliding in beside me. "By the way, good job with the tape across his mouth. The best part is nobody believes Brock Sullivan."

"Where did you…?" I started, but then I realized he could probably just appear out of thin air. Literally.

"This is going much better than I had planned," said Tom Sceal.

"Who called you?" I asked, trying to remain calm.

"Nobody calls me," the imp replied.

"Aren't you bound?" I asked. "Somebody must have called you out of the binding."

"You did some homework," Tom said with a laugh. "But not enough. Still, you've done better than I had hoped. Oh, look, here she comes." He pointed to the cafeteria door.

Jenna appeared in the doorway, looking for me, so I stood and waved to her with my right hand. With my left hand, I reached for Tom Sceal so he couldn't leave. But he was already gone.

"Darn it," I muttered as Jenna sat down.

"What's wrong?" Jenna asked.

"Tom Sceal was just here," I replied. "I wanted you to see him."

"He must be fast," said Jenna. "There was nobody beside you when you waved."

"Oh well," I said. Then I noticed the plastic container holding my brownie was open on the table, and the brownie was sparkling.

"Were you going to eat dessert first?" Jenna asked.

"No, I was saving that to share," I replied, looking around.

"Well, if it isn't the wicked witches," said Brock. "Where's your kettle?"

"Witches have cauldrons," I said, rolling my eyes.

"Like I care," said Brock. He leaned in and lowered his voice, "I'm going to get you back…"

"For what?" Jenna asked between bites.

"You know," said Brock. "It's gonna be payback time." Then he saw the brownie. He reached across both of us and grabbed it. "This is a good start."

"Hey!" Jenna reached for it, but I caught her hand. Jenna looked at me and frowned, then she hissed at Brock, "I hope you choke on it."

Brock laughed and walked off with a mouth full of chocolate.

"Why did you stop me?" said Jenna as I let go of her arm.

"Because I think Tom Sceal did something to that brownie," I replied. "I deliberately hid it in my bag so we could split it, but when you sat down, it was open and shimmering. Plus, once Brock touched it, I wasn't about to eat those germs."

"That's gross and true," said Jenna. "But if it's enchanted, I just told him I hoped he'd choke on it."

Across the playground, Brock started gagging very loudly. He fell to his knees and turned away from everybody so we couldn't see his face.

"Uh oh," Jenna said.

"Dude, don't be dramatic," Michael said as he hit Brock square between the shoulders.

A tiny frog hopped away from Brock.

A chorus of "Ewww" echoed around the playground. Then came the second frog and a third. A group of boys quickly tried to catch the frogs, leaving Brock completely alone.

In the chaos, most of the girls picked up their lunches and moved away.

Jenna spun around and looked at me with wide eyes. I know my mouth was open in shock.

"I am soooo glad we didn't eat that," Jenna said.

"Now we'll be called witches for sure," I said.

Out on the four-square court, Brock fell over onto his side, exhausted. Meanwhile, about twenty boys were chasing the frogs. A teacher came over and picked up Brock and walked him to the nurse's office.

"That's a lot of frogs for one brownie," I said.

"It does serve him right," said Jenna with a laugh.

"But you know we're going to pay for this," I replied, slumping.

"We didn't do anything," said Jenna. "That's the honest truth."

"I hope you're right," I said.

Of course, being right rarely counts when it comes to school stuff. Which explains why we were standing in Ms. Quinn's office about five minutes later.

"Honestly, we don't know what happened," Jenna said. Unfortunately for us, Ms. Quinn wasn't buying it. "Brock stole the brownie Ash's mom made for us."

"And then frogs jumped out of his mouth?" Ms. Quinn replied. "Just like that?"

"We're just two normal girls," said Jenna. "How could we…?"

"Well, Tom Sceal…" I started.

"Yes, I heard that Tom Sceal was back," Ms. Quinn interrupted. "Mrs. O'Shea and your mother warned me about him. What did he do?"

"He sat next to me while I was waiting for Jenna," I said. "And when he left, the brownie sparkled."

"You're telling me that a magical imp returned after thirty years and put a spell on a brownie that a Shannongale was going to share with her friend?" Ms. Quinn said more than asked. "And then the boy who likes to pick on you stole the brownie, ate it, and started coughing up frogs?"

"Yes, ma'am," I said as I turned my eyes downward. It was a bit unbelievable. No, actually, it was totally unbelievable.

"Ms. Quinn, we didn't do anything, honestly," said Jenna. "We couldn't believe it ourselves."

"The problem is that the whole school saw it, and tomorrow I might have to face dozens of parents — if not more — who will want an explanation," said Ms. Quinn. "And I don't have one. Do you think they'll believe me when I say a magical being showed up just a month after a new girl arrived at the school? Or that this imp decided to pick on one of the school's most notorious bullies?"

"Most adults don't believe in such things, do they?" I said, looking at my feet.

"Neither do most children," said Ms. Quinn. "They'll think it's you, and I can't have them thinking you two are witches."

"That wouldn't be good," said Jenna.

"Well, the nice thing is that nobody can connect you directly to Mr. Sullivan and the frogs," said the Principal. "From now on, you two are to stay far away from Brock Sullivan until this matter is settled. Do you understand?"

"Yes, ma'am," we said in unison.

"Ma'am?" continued Jenna. "We try to do that anyway. He's the one who comes after us."

"Somehow, I don't think he will anymore," said Ms. Quinn. "At least nobody saw a frog jump out of his mouth." She thought for a moment. "We'll say he was pulling another prank. Now, run along before I have to write a note to explain why you're late."

"Yes, ma'am," we said. We hurried out of the office just as the bell rang. Kids flooded the corridor, yelling and laughing. Jenna looked at me.

"What are we going to do now?" Jenna said.

"I don't know," I said. "I guess we'll see."

The class was quiet, probably because Brock wasn't there. During the afternoon recess, I went to the furthest picnic table from the playground, next to the cafeteria doors. I pulled out my sketchbook and began to draw Tom Sceal. I figured if I could make him tell me who he was working for, I could make this all stop.

"I'm going to get you," Brock Sullivan said with a hiss, his voice hoarse. He was standing next to my table when I looked up. "You'll be sorry you made me cough up frogs."

"I didn't do that," I said calmly. "Plus, you stole my brownie. I didn't do anything."

"That's a..." Brock thought about it, which I'm beginning to think is something new for him.

"Can I please just sit here quietly and draw?" I asked nicely.

"So, you want me to leave you alone?" Brock said, acting like it was an inconvenience.

"You were the one who walked all the way over here," I said. "You weren't anywhere close when I sat down."

"I was on my way..." Brock didn't know how to finish that defense.

"Please?" I sighed and put my head down.

"You're still a freak," said Brock. "And a witch."

"And you're still you," I said. "Fine, stay here. I'm going back to class," I said. "You can follow me if you want, but then everybody will think you like me."

"Ewww!" said Brock backing up. He spat on the ground. "That's just gross."

"I agree," I gathered my sketchbook and pencil.

CHAPTER FOURTEEN

Be Careful What You Wish For

After recess, Miss Desoto finally let us go to the library again to work on our projects. It was the lone bright spot in an otherwise difficult Thursday for me. Jenna and I snuck to the corner behind the shelves on magic and witchcraft, sat on the floor, and quietly worked on our project. I was drawing an old crone with a staff while Jenna was reading about the frog's leg strength.

"You know that a bullfrog can jump seven feet?" Jenna said quietly. "I wish I could jump that far."

"Me too," I said, and Jenna smiled.

"We should work on our project," said Jenna. "Do you think you could draw all the different phases of a bullfrog's life? Then we could show why people think they're magical."

"Oh, that's a great idea," I said. "What about this picture?" I pointed to a series of photographs showing frogs' eggs, a tadpole, a tadpole with legs, then a frog with a tail, and finally a full-grown frog.

"Perfect!" said Jenna with a big smile.

"I thought I smelled something bad," Brock said to Michael, who snickered.

"Why aren't you in the nurse's office," asked Jenna. "Or better yet, at the zoo?" Then she added, "Anywhere but here."

"They couldn't get a hold of my mom," said Brock. "Besides, I feel fine now."

"Which is why you came to bug us," Jenna replied. "How kind."

"You two freaks are the reason I coughed up frogs, and I know it," Brock said hoarsely.

"It sounds like you still have a frog in your throat," Jenna replied, which made me and Michael chuckle.

"What are you drawing?" Brock pointed to my rather good drawing of a bullfrog. "Another self-portrait?"

"You are such a jerk," Jenna said. "Can't you leave us alone? Ms. Quinn said you would."

"No, you're not getting off that easy," said Brock, his eyes narrowed as he scowled at Jenna.

I set down my pencil and looked up at the bully. I closed my eyes and counted to three before he interrupted me.

"Oh, did I hurt elf girl's feelings?" Brock said with a sneer.

"Hardly," I replied. "I was drawing... you." I tried to swallow that last word, but it escaped before I could stop myself. My eyes narrowed and turned golden. I felt the blood rush to my cheeks. I clenched my jaw and hissed, "Now, you better leave us alone before you start turning green."

Brock backed up quickly.

"Alright, no need to get so mad, geeze," he said. He bumped into Michael. "Get out of my way," he grumbled as he pushed past his one friend. Michael looked at me, swallowed hard, turned, and quickly followed Brock away. Jenna looked at me and put a hand on my shoulder.

"That was pretty scary." Jenna half chuckled.

"Sorry," I replied. "I just want him to leave us alone."

"Me too," said Jenna. "I think that worked."

"Ugh, he made me mess up my drawing," I looked at a stray line on my drawing. I pulled out my eraser and rubbed the mark away. "Some days, I do wish he was a frog so we wouldn't have to hear what he was saying," I said as I took in a breath and puffed out my cheeks.

"No, Aisling, don't blow!" But Jenna was too late. I was already halfway through blowing the erasing away.

"Uh oh," I said. We both looked at the drawing as it dissolved on the page. Above us, I heard a muffled laugh. I guess Jenna heard it too because we both looked up but didn't see anybody. It did smell like fresh rain, though.

"Oh no! What did I do?" I hung my head.

"Did the drawing dissolve when you blew on that drawing on the bus?" Jenna asked.

"I don't know," I said quietly but very scared. "We hurried off the bus, and I dropped the drawing." I looked at the paper. "What did I do?"

"Whatever happens, it's his own fault," said Jenna. "Maybe, hopefully, nothing will happen."

"Let's hope," I said, putting my hands to my mouth like I was going to pray. We leaned over and watched Brock race away from us and toward the middle of the library. We both cringed when Brock slammed into Tiffany Treacle. She was the one person even Brock wouldn't mess with.

"Oof!" they both exclaimed. The book Tiffany was holding flew out of her hands and slid under the nearby table.

Brock looked at us, real fear showing in his eyes.

"Excuse me," said Tiffany, putting her hands on her hips as she stood in front of Brock.

"You're excused," said Brock. He tried to keep going, but the Princesses blocked his path. "Oh, come on," he groaned.

"Pick it up," said Tiffany, indicating the book on the floor.

"What?" said Brock. Then he saw the book on the ground. "Sure, whatever."

He picked up the book and held it out for Tiffany. He turned to leave and let go of the book without looking, so it fell again.

"Seriously?" Tiffany said.

"You could at least try," Brock said as he bent to pick it up. Emma, the tallest of the Princesses, put her shoe on his back and pushed him down. He sprawled face-first on the library floor. The Princesses giggled.

"Hmmm, never mind," said Tiffany, stepping over Brock's body. "I was done with that one, anyway." She motioned with a head nod to the girls, and they turned in unison and walked to a large table in the center of the library.

Michael waited until the girls left before trying to help Brock. He bent down, picked up the book, and offered a hand to Brock. As Brock got back to his feet, he looked woozy. Brock let go of Michael's hand and leaned against the bookshelves. But he missed the metal shelf and pushed about six books onto the floor on the other side. I looked at Jenna. This wasn't a good sign.

"You okay, dude?" said Michael.

Brock shook his head no. Then he started to gag.

"You're not going to cough up more frogs?" Michael asked.

Brock clapped his hand to his mouth, pushed past Michael, and ran toward the bathroom.

Michael started to follow.

"Michael Jennings, where do you think you're going?" Ms. Clarke asked.

"I was…" the boy stammered. "Um, going to see if Brock is… okay."

"I think Mr. Sullivan can go to the bathroom by himself," replied Ms. Clarke. "I would suggest you stay here and clean up the mess you two made. Unless you want to risk detention."

"Yes, ma'am. No ma'am," Michael took one last look down the hall. The librarian motioned with her hand to the books on the floor between the shelves. Jenna looked at me.

"Uh oh," I said.

Michael returned to the shelves and picked up all the books. Then he looked at the librarian, not knowing what to do next.

"Place them in the cart," Ms. Clarke sighed. "I'll put them away properly."

Michael turned back to the librarian as he put the books in the library cart. "Um, where can I find a book on frogs?" he asked while still holding the book Tiffany originally had.

"In your hand," said Ms. Clarke. "Try reading it."

"What did we do?" Jenna whispered to me.

"I'm not sure," I said as I turned as white as a sheet of paper.

CHAPTER FIFTEEN

An Uneasy Peace

"I know I saw Brock Sullivan in the library. Has anybody seen him?" Miss Desoto asked. A bunch of hands shot up, but not mine or Jenna's. We turned and looked at each other.

"Yes, he was very rude and knocked a book out of my hand," said Tiffany Treacle with great satisfaction. She nodded as though this was the highest truth and most important detail.

"I'm sure he was," said Miss Desoto in that way she had of not dismissing, but at the same time stopping Tiffany and Brock.

"He said he wasn't feeling well," said Michael. "He ran to the bathroom, but I wasn't allowed to follow him. Maybe he went back to the nurse."

"Well, he's not with the nurse," said Miss Desoto. "Michael, will you go see if he's still in the boys' bathroom?"

"Yes, ma'am," said Michael, with a slight smile that he tried to hide.

"Don't dawdle, Mr. Jennings," said Miss Desoto. "The rest of you pull out your English books. Can anybody tell me what a metaphor is?"

A few hands shot up around class.

"Jenna, you're awfully quiet," said Miss Desoto. "What is a metaphor?"

"Um," Jenna stalled, obviously trying to refocus her thoughts. "It's a phrase that indirectly compares two things that are not alike but share some common characteristics."

"Excellent," said Miss Desoto. "Can anybody give me an example?"

"The computers in the library are dinosaurs," said Tiffany Treacle.

"Good, and another," said the teacher.

"They're like two peas in a pod," said Sophie, one of the Princesses.

"Actually, that's a simile," said Miss Desoto. "A simile makes the direct comparison, using words such as 'like' or 'as' to equate the two."

"She cried a river is a metaphor, and he ate like a pig is a simile," said Jenna.

"Perfect," said Miss Desoto.

As the discussion went on, I tried hard to think of examples, but the back of my mind was totally consumed by the possibility that I had turned Brock Sullivan into a frog. Then I began to worry. What if he hopped in front of a truck or car? What if he got eaten by another animal? I would be responsible for killing Brock! I started to feel like I was going to throw up.

"Miss Desoto," I raised my hand meekly. "May I be excused for a minute?"

"Yes, Aisling," said the teacher. "Please hurry back."

"Yes, ma'am," I said, then I nodded to Jenna to say that I was fine. But I wasn't. I walked quickly and calmly out of the class and ran straight to the girls' room. The tears broke through about five steps from the girls' bathroom. I rushed to the sink and ran some cold water. Then I splashed my face. I still felt pretty queasy as I pulled a paper towel to dry my hands and face. I looked at the paper towel and got an idea.

I grabbed a dry paper towel and went into the furthest bathroom stall from the door. I locked the stall door and pulled a small pencil from my pocket. I began to draw Brock as a boy. As soon as it looked kind of like him, I thought about wanting him back to normal and blew on the drawing.

It did not sparkle or vanish. I groaned and hung my head.

"Aisling?" Jenna said, opening the door. "Are you okay?"

"Yeah… no," I said from the stall. "Think I'm going to be sick."

"It's not your fault," said Jenna. "Can you come back to class? Miss Desoto sent me to check on you."

"Yeah," I said as I crumpled up the drawing and shoved it into my pocket. I opened the stall and came out. I washed my hands and splashed my face again, then dried with another paper towel. I threw away the drawing and the wet towel and looked at Jenna.

"Honestly," said Jenna. "It's not your fault. Besides, we don't even know what happened."

"Yeah," I said, looking in the mirror. "Maybe he just didn't feel well after coughing up frogs." I think we both knew that was a lie.

"You sure you're okay? We better go back to class so Tiffany Treacle doesn't come looking for us," said Jenna.

"That would make things worse," I said. "I'm okay," I lied again. I still felt horrible, and I knew it showed. I just couldn't hide anything, it seemed.

We walked back to class, but I just kept feeling worse. When we got back to the room, Miss Desoto took one look at us and immediately ordered me to the nurse's office.

About fifteen minutes later, my mom showed up.

"What's up, buttercup?" Mom asked as she knelt in front of me.

"I don't feel good," I said quite honestly. But I couldn't even raise my eyes to meet my mom's gaze.

"Alright, let's go home," said mom. "I'll sign you out." We left the school and walked to the car in silence. Just before she started the engine, mom turned to me. "What happened?" she asked as she reached over and put her hand on my shoulder.

"I think I turned Brock into a frog," I replied.

"Oh dear," replied her mother, putting both hands on the wheel and turning to look out of the windshield. "Are you sure?"

"No, but pretty sure," I sniffed. "And that makes me a bigger bully than he is! I mean, what if I killed..."

And that was it. I had kept it together as long as I could. The tears raced to my eyes, bringing with them deep sobs. Huge drops formed in the corners and even on the lashes of my eyes. I put my hands to my face, leaned forward, and collapsed.

Mom rubbed my back and then reached for the key in the ignition.

"Let's get you home. There we can talk about it safely and see what we can do," she said as she started the car.

I nodded as I gasped for air.

"It's okay. Let it out, honey," mom said. "Trust me, Ash, you are not a bully." Mom checked her surroundings and pulled out of the parking lot. "But we need to make this right."

CHAPTER SIXTEEN

Practicing Magic

"We've got to get your magic under control," my mom said as we walked straight into the kitchen. "Let's start by creating some happy, easy magic. Get out your sketchbook."

"But Mom…" I looked at her in horror. Yeah, let's potentially kill somebody else. Always a good idea. What was she thinking? "When I went to the bathroom, I tried to draw Brock as a boy, and I blew on it, but nothing happened."

"Did you draw in your sketchbook?" Mom asked.

"No, on a paper towel," I said. "Wait! You mean it's enchanted only if I draw in my sketchbook?"

"Maybe," said Mom. "Try it now and see."

I pulled out my sketchbook while Mom grabbed some paper and pencils. I picked up a pencil and drew Brock as a boy, just like

I did yesterday, but without the tape over his mouth. I showed it to my mom, then blew on it. It shimmered and disappeared off the page.

"Is that what happened when you blew on the frog in the library?" Mom asked.

"Yup," I said. "Does that mean it worked?"

"I'm not sure," Mom said. "Let's test something where we can see the results." She looked around the room. "Why don't you draw a vase and some flowers for the kitchen table."

I nodded, then bent over the page and focused on creating tulips and daffodils for her table. I drew a simple vase for them with a bow around it. I looked up when I finished, and my mother smiled and nodded. "Now blow on it," she said.

I blew on the drawing. Just like the picture of Brock, it shimmered, then disappeared. But nothing happened. Rats, I thought, and I scrunched up my forehead, trying to understand.

"Guess it didn't work," I said.

"Did Brock turn into a frog instantly?"

"No, he bumped into Tiffany Treacle," I replied. "Maybe it takes time…"

The doorbell rang, and somebody knocked loudly.

I looked toward the door and swallowed hard. It was probably the police coming to question me about Brock. What was I going to say? I didn't do it on purpose. And how did they know it was me? I don't want to go to jail. Mom got up to see who it was while I stared at the now blank page in my sketchbook. They'd probably confiscate my sketchbook as evidence. I'd never be allowed to draw in prison!

I slumped forward until Mom returned and set down a blue vase full of tulips and daffodils, just like I drew. Even the arrangement was exactly like my sketch, down to the bow around the vase. I looked at her.

"There was no note," said Mom. "Just the flowers that you drew."

We sat and looked at the flowers and vase. I know my mouth was hanging open. Mom leaned in and smelled the flowers, and finally smiled.

"Okay, we know your magic is real," she said. "It just doesn't always work instantly." She paused and looked around the room. "Alright, let's try the regular paper. Ash, what would you like?"

"I could use some cake and ice cream," I said as I almost smiled through my exhaustion. Who knew that thinking you might have turned a bully into a bullfrog was so exhausting?

"Okay, let's draw that," my mom laughed.

I grinned for the first time that afternoon, closed my eyes, and drew a big piece of cake with ice cream on top. When I finished, I looked at Mom for approval.

"That's a lot of cake, but I think we can split it," she said. "Alright, now blow on it."

I took a deep breath and blew on the drawing. It shimmered a bit but stayed in place on the paper. I looked over at the counter, but no cake appeared. I got up and ran to the door. Nobody was pulling up to deliver a cake. I went back to the kitchen and opened the fridge, but there was still no cake. I frowned.

"Well, that's good to know," Mom said.

"But I still want some cake!" I said, faking a pout.

"Me too!" Mom laughed, then said, "Let's try something different." She quickly scrolled through her phone. "I want you to draw this pair of wooden clogs in your sketchbook, but this time I want you to focus on the cake you want." She held up a picture of clogs on her phone.

"Okay," I said. I closed my eyes and focused on the cake. I could almost taste the chocolatey goodness. Then I started to draw the clogs. They were pretty easy to draw, which meant I could focus on thinking about eating cake. I sketched in the flowers that were painted on the clogs and some shadows. When I finished, I blew on the page.

It shimmered, then disappeared. I looked at mom expectantly. Then something banged in the fridge.

"That was probably the ice-maker," she said, but I was already opening the door. I screamed, then laughed.

"What is it, Ash?" said Mom.

"This!" I pulled out two cakes in the shape of clogs, with flowers made from frosting.

"Well, that could be dangerous," Mom said, looking concerned.

"Getting two cakes is dangerous?" I said, laughing.

"You combined two things, Ash," she said. "What if you draw a wolf and think of your friend?"

"She could turn into a wolf?" I said, my smile fading.

"Or she could meet a wolf," Mom said. "Neither is good. Hmmm." She paused to think. "Put one clog cake back in the fridge and bring the other one over here."

I beamed as I carried the cake to the table. I stopped on the way and picked two forks from the silverware drawer, then set the cake down in the middle of the table, between us. Naturally, I focused on what would be the best first bite to take.

"One more experiment first," Mom said.

CHAPTER SEVENTEEN

The Rules of Magic

"I want you to draw the kitten that you've always wanted," mom said. "But don't blow on it. I want to see if the magic only works if you blow on it immediately after you finish."

"Okay!" my smile returned. This could end up being a great day, especially if Brock got home safely. I picked up my sketchbook and drew a fluffball of a kitten with pointy ears, a tiny nose, big bright eyes, and his head cocked a bit to the right. I showed it to mom.

"Boy or girl?" she asked.

"Boy, I think," I replied.

"Well, he is beautiful," mom said. "What's his name?"

"Hmmm." I thought for a second, then smiled. "Coven," I declared. "Because everybody thinks I'm a witch now."

"That makes sense," my mom said with a wink. "And Coven will be your familiar."

"What is a familiar?" I asked, still focused on the finishing touches of my kitten. "I keep reading that word in our research."

"It's an animal that assists a witch in creating magic," replied my mom with a smile. "Even an imp like Tom Sceal can be a familiar, if the witch is powerful enough to control him."

"I don't think anybody could control him," I sighed.

"Yet somebody does," said mom. "And that witch or sorcerer must be very powerful."

"But I'm not a witch, am I?" I asked, looking at my mother with concern.

"No, honey," she said, grinning. "You're a good part elf, so equally magical in some ways. But it never hurts to have an assistant."

"Like a magical pet?" I asked.

"Exactly," smiled mom. "Now, put the kitten drawing aside, and let's hope this clog cake doesn't taste like your shoes smell."

"Ewww!" I was almost afraid to try the cake.

Mom dipped her fork into the clog cake and pulled out a small bite. The cake was pink on the inside with white frosting. The flowers were different colors of frosting. My mouth watered as I watched mom enjoy her first bite.

"Mmm. Magic always tastes amazing!" she half moaned in delight.

"Wait, you've tasted magic before?" I said as I lifted the fork to my mouth. My bite was a brown and red cake with the same white frosting. It looked so different from my mom's forkful, but I shrugged and put it in my mouth.

"Tell me what you taste," mom said, nodding.

An explosion of flavors filled my mouth. Raspberries and nuts and vanilla and chocolate all danced around on my tongue.

"Wow!" I said with my mouth full. I chewed and swallowed. "It was like… and then… mmmm."

"Exactly," mom said. "But, I'll bet you ended with something chocolate."

"I did!" I nodded as I took another bite. "I made a chocolate cake!" But there were so many flavors swirling around in my mouth.

"Well, my bites taste like strawberry cheesecake," Mom said as she carved herself another small bite.

"How is that possible?" I asked before I took my third bite.

"How is any of this possible?" she replied. "It's magic."

"Do you still have the magic Tom Sceal gave you?" I asked.

"Well, here's the thing," said my mom. "He didn't give you magic. He just unlocked it."

"What do you mean?" I asked before putting another forkful in my mouth.

"Every Shannongale woman has magic," mom said. "But we can't use it until just before we turn eleven. It's to keep us safe until we're old enough to learn to control it."

"So, my drawing skill won't wear off?" I asked.

"No," she replied. "But it will take a lot of hard work and focus to bring your magic under control. I didn't have magic that I could do by accident," she added. "I have to wave my hand above my head."

"Like you do every morning at the art festival?"

"You noticed," mom replied with a wink.

"I always knew you had magic," I said. "But you always had an explanation."

"Sometimes when it was hard to hide it from you," she said.

"I wish it was harder for me to do accidental magic," I replied. "Do you think I could do a spell to make it harder?"

"Using magic to control magic rarely works," she replied. "Three things could happen. One, it could work, and that would be great. Or two, and more likely, it would backfire, and you would have even less control."

"What's number three?" I asked.

"Three," mom looked closely at me. "You could have all of your blocks restored, so you lose all your magic and just be a normal girl."

"I don't know that number three is so bad," I said, thinking back to when I realized what happened to Brock. "But I don't ever want to be a bully again, mom."

"You weren't a bully," said mom. "You made a mistake. Being a bully is not in your heart."

"Well, after being picked on at two schools, I think that me being a normal girl would require magic." I took another bite of cake and savored it.

"You wouldn't be able to make magic cake," mom shrugged and smiled.

"But you still could," I replied.

"Perhaps," said mom. "But, when you reverse things, you might lose the ability to draw again."

"Oh," I stopped. "You think… Seriously?"

"There's a chance," said mom. "But the worst thing would be that the spell would backfire."

"What do you mean?

"Undoing magic with more magic can actually make things worse," said mom. "Fortunately, our magic only lasts until the sun sets or rises. Any mistakes are fixed the next day."

"So, this cake and those flowers will be gone tonight?" I asked.

"They might be," said mom. "Some things stay, and some things go. I am still figuring out that logic."

"But what if Brock gets run over or eaten while he's a frog?" I started to worry again.

"Trust me, Tom Sceal is watching over him carefully," replied mom. "His job is to teach a bully a lesson, not hurt or kill him."

"Are you sure?" I asked. I looked at my mom, wondering how she could be calm.

"I have it on the very best authority," she smiled.

CHAPTER EIGHTEEN

What's Done Is Done

I waited by the door to the school for the first bell of the morning to ring. Brock was still nowhere to be seen. I also hadn't seen Jenna, who usually ran off some energy and kicked the ball before class.

To be honest, all I wanted to do was go home and play with Coven. The little black furball had wandered into our backyard just after we finished the cake. He mewed loudly at the kitchen door until we let him in. The best part was that Coven didn't disappear when the sun set. In fact, he slept on my bed and looked at me like I was crazy when I got out of bed that morning for school.

"Cute cat," said Tom Sceal as he snuck up behind me. Again! I jumped, then rolled my eyes. I was so lost in thought that I had completely missed the smell of rain.

"How did you... Never mind. Did you take care of Brock?" I asked or perhaps demanded.

"Don't worry so much, Aisling Shannongale," said Tom Sceal with his trademark grin. "We had a grand time. Ask him how the banquet of flies tasted."

"Eww, gross," I winced. Okay, maybe Brock deserved that.

"It was glorious," Tom Sceal chuckled. "Wish you could have seen it. Too bad you turned him back to normal when you did. I thought he might like some minnow sushi." He paused for a second, then added, "You know, I thought maybe that sneaky Tiffany Treacle could use a lesson."

"No, no more lessons," I said. The bell erupted above us, and when I looked back, Tom Sceal was gone.

The kids filed into the building and up the stairs. Then they scattered to their classes like bees at a hive. I took my seat in Room 222, but Jenna wasn't beside me. I looked up at Miss Desoto's desk, but she wasn't there either. I began to worry. What if Brock had blamed Jenna, and Jenna was in trouble instead of me? And what if Brock's parents blamed Miss Desoto?

The door opened and in strode a very stern older woman. The class fell silent as she marched up to the desk, set down her purse and small briefcase, then looked around. She went to the board and printed her name on it. "My name is Ms. Ersatz. Miss Desoto called in sick today, and I will be your substitute teacher. I have your lesson plan, and we *will* accomplish everything on it. Do I make myself clear?"

"Yes, ma'am," said the class, rather unenthusiastically. Ms. Ersatz pulled her reading glasses and a piece of paper from her briefcase. The glasses were half-height, allowing her to read and look over the top. She ran through the first half of the class attendance, with everybody saying, "Here."

"Jenna Healy?" asked Ms. Ersatz. Nobody answered, so I raised my hand. "Are you Jenna?"

"No, ma'am. But Jenna usually sits here," I indicated the seat next to me. "I haven't seen her today."

"Very well, seems to be a bit of that going around," the teacher marked on the paper. "Michael Jennings," the teacher asked.

"Present," said Michael.

"Emma Lemmon?" Ms. Ersatz half asked, half announced.

"Here," said Emma with a perfect Princess smile.

"A... Aiz... ling..." she tried.

"It's pronounced Ash-leen, ma'am," I said. "Aisling Shannongale, and I am here."

"So you are," Ms. Ersatz said, looking over the paper. The teacher paused and studied me and my red hair before continuing down the list.

"Brock Sullivan?" she said. Nobody answered. "Sullivan? Brock?" she asked again.

The door yanked opened and in walked a very grumpy Brock.

"I'm here," he grumbled. "But I don't want to sit near that witch ever again!" He pointed to me, and the class murmured.

I looked down because my face was suddenly feeling like it was going to burst into flames.

"That is a horrible thing to say," said the teacher. "Now, apologize and take your seat immediately."

"I'm not apologizing," said Brock. "She turned me into a frog."

"Oh, you must be Mr. Sullivan," said Ms. Ersatz said, putting down the attendance list. "I was warned about you. They said you had quite the imagination."

"It's true!" Brock shouted.

"Well, you look and sound exactly the way I imagined you when Mrs. O'Shea described you."

"Well, I changed back," said Brock, and the class laughed.

"And we're delighted you did," said Ms. Ersatz, looking at the attendance sheet. "Tiffany Treacle?"

"Here, Ms. Ersatz," said Tiffany with her incredibly fake smile. The teacher smiled back at the girl.

The teacher ran through the last four names. When she finished, she asked Tiffany Treacle to take the list to Mrs. O'Shea, which Tiffany was perfectly proud to do.

The rest of the morning went by rather quickly, which surprised me. To be honest, Ms. Ersatz scared me even more than Miss Desoto inspired me to be a good student. When the recess bell rang, I felt like I had taken a deep breath for the first time since that substitute had walked through the door. I grabbed my sketchbook and headed outside.

I found a picnic table far away from the kids running around. Brock or anybody else would have to be seriously looking for me to find me here. I pulled out my sketchbook and drew dots in the four corners for a Zen doodle. I stretched out my hand, pushing my fingers as far apart as I could. I was really tense. I sighed and took a deep breath, which is when I smelled fresh rain again.

"Not you again," I said.

"You don't like me anymore?" said Tom as he sat beside me.

"You... this... this magic scared me to death," I said. "And now Brock is convinced that I'm a witch."

"But you're not a witch," said Tom Sceal. "I work with witches all the time..."

"That doesn't matter," I said. "I can do magic, and that would make me a witch in almost anybody's eyes."

"You can do magic because I enchanted your notebook," said Tom Sceal.

"Yes! But they don't know that. And I'm tired of worrying," I said. "I don't want my drawings turning into real-life if I accidentally blow on them."

"Even your flowers, your cake, and your kitten?"

"Were you spying on me?" I asked.

"No, but I am, shall we say, 'notified' every time you use your enchantment," Tom said. "Besides, I was busy babysitting a frog."

"Stop it," I said. "I just want to be a normal girl."

"Oh, Aisling Shannongale, it has been ordained for centuries before you were born that you would be anything but a normal girl," said Tom Sceal with a smile. "You are a Shannongale. A halfling born on the summer solstice. Otherwise, my enchantment would not have worked."

"Wait. What? Ordained?" I paused, then shook my head. "Never mind. You're trying to confuse me, and the stuff you're talking about doesn't matter. I'm going to draw me needing to wave my arms over my head like my mom," I said. "I want control over what turns into magic."

"You can't just wish for that," said Tom, shaking his head.

"Why not?" I replied, more as a dare than a question. I began drawing myself in my sketchbook.

"The magic works with you and through you," said Tom. "You adapt to it, not the other way around."

"Then undo it," I said, getting mad.

"What's done is done," said Tom Sceal, his smile fading. "I can't undo it, and neither can you. And you can't go back in time to undo it."

"Says who?" I said as I drew myself, sitting at the picnic table.

"It was written long ago," said Tom, watching me as I shaded in the drawing. "Before we wrote letters. When the humans and the fae worked together."

"A rule being old doesn't make it good," I said. I looked at Tom Sceal with an I-don't-care smile. I finished the drawing and held it up for him to see.

"I wouldn't do that," said Tom Sceal.

CHAPTER NINETEEN

Overdoing the Undo

"Why not?" I almost shouted. "Are you afraid you'll have to do the spells yourself?" I lifted the page to my mouth.

"At best, you will lose your ability to draw the way you want," said Tom, and I lowered the drawing. "Look back in your sketchbook," he continued as the pages turned by themselves. "Do you want to go back to that style?"

"No," I said, setting down my sketchbook.

"Do you want your kitten to be missing when you get home today?" Tom Sceal's impish grin faded. He looked surprisingly serious and even threatening. "Do you want the cake you brought for lunch to disappear?"

"But why can't I be semi-normal?" I asked. "I don't want to hurt anybody."

"Your family has never been 'normal' or even semi-normal," Tom said, using air quotes around the word normal. "Shannongale women have always been suspected of being witches or being somehow magical by humans. And you are the most special of your kind."

"What do you mean, 'most special of my kind'?" I asked. "I'm just a regular kid."

"Your ears say otherwise," replied Tom Sceal.

"You're mean," I said, pulling my hair over my ears. "You're a bully, and you're turning me into an even worse one than Brock."

"Well, you are half-right," said Tom Sceal. "I am a bully, but not just like them. I come to teach them a lesson, and I do find my job fun. As for you, your heart is too pure for you to become a bully."

"Who sent you?" I insisted.

"Ahh, now you know I can't tell you that," smiled the imp. "Only my mistress can reveal herself."

"You mean you *are* a witch's familiar?"

"Ha! I am far more powerful than that, my young friend," said Tom Sceal. "And far less predictable."

I looked down and frowned at the simple drawings of a kitten and a frog. I turned the page to the beautiful illustration of the frog. I swallowed hard and wiped the tear forming in the corner of my eye. I flipped to the drawing of myself, then closed my eyes and held up my sketchbook.

"Well, I'm done being your puppet," I said.

"Please don't," Tom covered the book with his hand as I was about to blow on my drawing.

"Why not?" I asked. "Afraid you'll lose your power over me?"

"No," the imp replied with a stern look. "I'm more afraid that you'll lose your power over you. There's a better chance your magic will backfire in a big way. And you don't want that."

"What do you mean, backfire?" I asked.

"Your magic will most likely grow stronger," said Tom sternly. "You are trying to multiply magic on top of magic. That never goes well. It could get out of control very fast."

"What happened the last time a spell like this backfired?" I asked.

"The potato crop failed, and more than a million people starved in the old country. It was almost two hundred years ago," said Tom Sceal. "All because one girl like you was tired of eating potatoes. You can look it up."

"That's not going to happen," I said.

"You're rather confident," said Tom Sceal. "So was she. Too much so. Magic is something you know nothing about."

"Well, I'm willing to risk it if it means I never have to spend another day thinking I killed somebody," I said.

"Let me get this straight. You are willing to give up your magic to spare a bully from learning a lesson? This kid has made your life a living nightmare since you got here," Tom Sceal almost pleaded with me. "A bully who, by the way, you never put in danger because I was always watching."

"But you let me think I did," I said. "So, tell me this valuable lesson Brock had to learn."

"The lesson is, when you bully others, there is always somebody more powerful than you," said Tom Sceal. "True power comes from within. It comes from caring, not from threatening and teasing."

I had to admit, that would be a good lesson for Brock to learn. But still.

"Why do I have to be the teacher of that lesson?" I asked. "I'm a nobody here."

"You're the perfect teacher," said Tom Sceal. "Because you know what it's like to be bullied."

"Yeah, and now you're turning me into one," I replied.

"I'm sorry for that," said Tom Sceal. "Just let me finish what I've started, and I'll let you be."

"No. You're going to let me be now," I said. "I don't want this magic."

I blew on the drawing. It shimmered, then vanished.

"No!" shouted Tom Sceal.

"Phooey, you're still here," I said, totally not believing his threats. "I guess it didn't work. I haven't done anything, have I?"

My voice trailed off as I looked at my hands, which were shimmering. Even my hair and shirt seemed to vibrate. I looked down and saw my jeans and shoes flash too.

"Oh dear, now you've done it," sighed Tom.

"What's happening?" I cried.

"I told you it would most likely backfire," said the imp. He took a deep breath, then looked at me. "Plus, you wished for a negative."

"What are you talking about?" I could feel my heart racing. Every cell in my body was vibrating. My ears started ringing.

"You have to wish for what you want," said Tom Sceal. "Not what you don't want. Magic doesn't understand words like 'don't' and 'not' and 'no.' It gets confused and often does the opposite of what you want."

"You need to teach people how to use this stuff before you make them magical!" I shouted. "How was I to know?"

"I warned you," said Tom Sceal. "You brought this on yourself."

"What's happening?" My voice shook as my body started rising above the table. I dropped my pencil and grabbed the edge of the bench to hold on so I wouldn't float away.

"*Ar ais go talamh*," whispered Tom Sceal, waving his hand in front of me.

"Back to earth?" I asked, not knowing how I understood his gibberish.

"Ahh, I guess one of your new powers is that you understand Gaelic now," Tom smiled again. "Well, let's see what else you did," Tom said as he put his index finger in his mouth and pulled it out. Then he scanned me with his finger like he was using one of those wands at the airport. "Just as I feared," Tom Sceal said. "There's no control."

"What?" I stood up, then sat down immediately. My whole body felt tingly, and my legs were a bit wobbly. "What do you mean there's no control?"

"There's no control on your magic," said Tom Sceal. "Your mother has to wave her hands. You had to blow on the paper. Now all you need do is set your mind. It seems that if you move your finger, you might be able to focus your magic," he added. "But you don't have to draw or blow anymore."

"How long will this last?" I asked.

"Most enchantments will last until the sun touches the sea," said Tom Sceal, then he put his finger up again to scan her. "Well, some of your enchantments will. You, well, oh dear… Hmmm…"

"What do you mean?" I demanded. "Stop speaking in riddles."

"You made yourself much more powerful," Tom said. "Anything you think of you can make real with your intent."

"In my sketchbook?" I asked, pushing away my beautiful and now shimmering sketchbook.

"Now, you see, I only enchanted your sketchbook," said Tom Sceal. "I simply made it, so you had to blow life into your magic. But you… You just enchanted yourself."

"Are you serious?" I looked at my hands, which were shaking. When I looked up, Tom Sceal was gone. I swallowed hard. Why didn't I listen to him and my mom? Ugh.

What was I going to do now?

CHAPTER TWENTY

The Magic Exchange

"There's the witch," said a voice that could only be Brock. I pretended not to notice, but I pulled back my sketchbook, just in case, and watched him from under my hair. "I swear she turned me into a frog yesterday," the boy said.

"Yeah, right," said Michael.

"It's true!" Brock turned red-faced. "There was a zookeeper waiting in the bathroom, and he took me to a pond and made me eat flies."

"Do you know how crazy that sounds?" Michael shook his head, then turned and walked away.

"I'm not crazy! Take that back!" Brock yelled as he chased after his friend. When he caught up, he looked like he was going to explode. "Or I swear…"

"Fine, I take it back," said Michael. "But that won't change it."

I smiled to myself a bit, then opened my sketchbook and started another Zen doodle.

"Those are fine to draw," said Tom Sceal. "Since you insisted on playing with magic, here are a few rules you must understand. First, the magic works through you. Not for you, not beside you, through you. You need to understand and choose what kind of magic you want to make in this world."

"Okay," I said as I swallowed hard.

"And you must remember that magic is an exchange," added the imp. "Your drawings used to pay the price."

"My drawings?" Aisling replied, looking up.

"Yes," said Tom. "They disappeared. You transformed all the attention, skill, and energy you put into each drawing into magic. But now..." He paused and studied the girl before he continued. "Now, you must consider the exchange."

"Like what?" I asked.

"Well, magic requires energy," said Tom Sceal. "Just say you wanted an ice-cream truck right now. It would have to come from somewhere. And maybe some other kids would miss out on ice cream. Or the driver would miss being with his sick mother or something."

"I don't want that."

"What if you want a million dollars?" said the imp. "Where would that come from?"

"The bank?" I answered.

"Most likely," said Tom Sceal. "But wouldn't that be stealing?"

I pondered all of this for a minute. I rubbed my forehead, then ran my fingers through my hair.

"You mean magic is stealing?" I asked.

"It can be," said Tom Sceal. "Dark magic steals energy from somewhere. But light magic is more of a trade. You trade one thing for another."

"Like my drawings," I said.

"Exactly," said Tom Sceal.

"What did you trade to enchant my sketchbook?"

"That was a good deed," replied Tom Sceal. "I gave you a gift. That was the exchange. I transformed all the energy you put into your drawings before to unlock your natural ability to draw the way you see. And you have used that gift for good — you saved a kitten, you taught a bully a lesson, you shared your cake with your mother, and you created some beautiful pictures that you can share with the class. Those are good things."

"How is making Brock cough up frogs a good thing?" I frowned and wrinkled my nose at the idea.

"Actually, that was me," replied the imp with a devilish smile. "I enchanted the brownie your mother made because I knew he would steal it."

"What if I had shared it with Jenna?" I asked. I crossed my arms defiantly.

"Shared what with me?" asked Jenna, plopping down next to me. "Sorry I'm late."

"I'm so glad to see you," I said and hugged my friend. "I thought you were in trouble or something had happened to you!"

"Aww, no. I just had to go to the dentist," said Jenna. "Regular checkup. Did Brock return to his human form?"

"Fortunately, and unfortunately," I replied. "Still, nobody believes him, so that's good."

"Phew!" Jenna pretended to wipe her brow. "How are you going to get this magic stuff under control?"

"My mom and I did some experiments last night," I said. "But I think I just made it worse."

"What do you mean, worse?" Jenna asked.

"I tried to undo all the magic, and now this…" I held up my pencil, and my hand sparkled. Jenna leaned back and looked at me.

"Whoa," said Jenna. "You're kinda shimmering."

"Tom Sceal said that all I have to do now is think of something and move my finger, and my thoughts become things," I said softly.

"Wow…" said Jenna cautiously. "Is that good?"

"I guess we'll find out," I replied. "But it scares me. There's some sort of trade-off."

"Okay, this is intense. I need to get a snack first," Jenna said. "I didn't eat before the dentist."

"What would you like?" I asked.

"I wish I had a strawberry muffin. Why?" Jenna asked. I smiled and drew a muffin in my book and wiggled my finger at it.

Jenna jumped back. Then she reached into her trainer jacket pocket and pulled out a strawberry muffin. "You didn't even blow?" she said.

"But I did exchange the drawing for the muffin," I said, holding up the blank page as Jenna wolfed down her muffin.

"Thanks, I was starving," she said as the first bell sounded.

"We have a substitute today," I warned Jenna while we walked to class.

"Ms. Ersatz?" Jenna said.

"You know her?" I asked.

"Yeah, she's subbed before," replied Jenna. "She's not as mean as she looks."

We got to class and took our seats. Brock wheeled around to glare at me, so I just rolled my eyes at him.

"Mr. umm…" Ms. Ersatz looked at the class sheet. "Mr. Sullivan, would you like to look this way? I realized the pretty girl behind you might be a distraction, but your test scores indicate that looking at her is not going to help you pass this grade."

"She's not pretty," said Brock. "She's a witch."

"There will be no name-calling," said Ms. Ersatz. "Now, apologize."

"Sorry," mumbled Brock loud enough for the teacher to hear. Then under his breath, he added, "Witch."

As the late morning trundled on, I probably spent as much time wondering how I could control my new magic as I did listening in class. I figured that if I could just focus on the trade, that might help.

Ms. Ersatz covered math, vocabulary, and spelling, none of which I was any good at. Add to that how my world had been turned upside down so many times this past week, and I think I should be forgiven for having a doubly hard time focusing.

On top of that, it seemed Brock had decided farting was about the best revenge he could get. Or maybe he was having a hard time digesting the flies he had eaten for dinner last night. Either way, each fart was progressively worse. The kids on either side of him and behind him were all waving papers and books to waft the smell away.

My eyes were watering. Without thinking, I wished somebody would put a cork in his butt. Of course, that thought came just before I tried to spell '*onomatopoeia*.' I touched my pencil to the page, and Brock let out an "eep!" I tried not to pay attention to it because I was busy holding my nose with my left hand while writing with my right.

"Ms. Ersatz," said James, who sat next to Brock. "May I open the window? I think somebody pooped their pants."

"Oh dear," said the teacher indicating that James could open the window. "Does somebody need to go to the bathroom?" Brock wiggled uncomfortably in his chair. "Mr. Sullivan, is it safe to assume that you need to be excused?"

"Yes, ma'am," Brock squeaked. He stood up and shuffled to the door, clearly trying to hold in something.

"Hurry along," Ms. Ersatz said.

Brock rushed out the door as the class laughed. The kids around him breathed an overly dramatic sigh of relief as fresh air from the opened window resuscitated the room. I looked up and realized what I might have done. I looked to Jenna and mouthed, *uh oh*.

Had I put a cork in his…? No, not again! I truly was a bully. I wished that Brock was okay and that his stomach pain had disappeared. Then I turned back to my spelling words, closed my eyes to focus, and wrote '*restore*' on the page. My hand shimmered.

I quickly looked around, but everybody was heads-down, working on their spelling.

A couple minutes later, Brock slipped back into class quietly, which was unusual. He glared at me but sat down and focused on the spelling and vocabulary words. I guess he took care of what was causing the rest of us pain because he didn't create any new odors for the remainder of the morning.

When the lunch recess bell rang, Brock turned to say something, but I got up first and turned my back on him.

"I hope the room airs out," Jenna said, looking behind me at Brock. "Maybe the janitor can sanitize it."

We both brought our lunches, so we grabbed a table far from the cafeteria door.

"What the heck was going on with Brock there?" Jenna asked as we sat down.

"I think he was having a hard time digesting frog food," I said with a grimace.

"Yeah, that's pretty gross," Jenna said as she winced and shook her head.

"His farts were giving me a headache," I replied.

"He's not having a good day, is he?" said Jenna.

"I'll show you who's going to have a crappy day!" Brock's hand grabbed my sketchbook and held it out of reach.

My mouth dropped open as Brock looked at the leather-bound book while keeping an eye on the two of us.

"Don't come any closer," he said, holding up his finger. "I'll rip it to shreds."

CHAPTER TWENTY-ONE

Truth or Dare

"Give it back!" I barked loudly as I stepped closer. "My mom gave that to me, and so help me...'

"This is how you make your magic, isn't it, witch?" he smirked. He flipped through the pages.

"Do you see any spells or magic in there?" I demanded. "Look through it. Do you see anything magical?"

"There are lots of drawings of frogs and witches in here," he jutted out his jaw in victory.

"Our class project is on frogs, you idiot," Jenna replied. "But you probably didn't know that."

"I knew," Brock said defiantly. "I just..."

"The truth is, we were writing a paper on frogs and magic," I said. "And you kept bugging us, so we teased you back. That's all!"

"But, the frogs!" Brock stammered.

"I swear, if you wreck the last bit of art for our project, I'll kick you from here to the frog pond myself," said Jenna.

"Give back my book before you ruin it!" I screamed as loud as I could.

The playground fell silent as everybody turned to look at Brock and me. Great. Now I was the center of attention, too.

"There's nothing in there about you," I snarled.

"Doesn't matter," yelled Brock. "I'm still gonna tear it up so you can't do magic or your stupid drawings anymore," he screamed at me.

"You better not!" I roared. I knew my eyes were turning gold again, and that was not a good thing. I couldn't have things catching fire right now. The teachers at Oakville Academy couldn't blame me when things went wrong, but they did. It was why nobody got into trouble for bullying me.

I kept looking Brock in the eyes as I fought to control my breath. Jenna stood up and slowly moved to the side.

"Or what?" said Brock, escalating the threats.

"Honestly, I'll show you that I don't need the sketchbook to teach you a lesson..." I growled. Brock backed up. Something clicked inside. *Honestly.* That's it! I smirked at the bully. "You think eating flies is bad... I'll make you eat your lies." I lowered my head like a lioness as I slowly advanced, almost stalking him like prey.

"What? You wouldn't..." Brock didn't seem as sure. He backed up a bit.

"Do you really want to find out?" I asked as I took another step forward. "Imagine how every lie you tell tastes."

"Baloney!" shouted Brock. He reached into the sketchbook and tore out a page of frogs I had drawn.

"Oh, you've done it now, doofus," Jenna said as Brock looked at me.

My eyes were now glowing gold like fire. I held out my hand behind me, and a pencil flew into it. I moved my hand in front of me and held the pencil like a sword.

"Brock, this is not going to end well for you," Jenna said and shook her head. "Can't you see?" I growled and stomped my foot on the ground in frustration.

"How'd you do that?" Brock pointed to the pencil. "You *are* using magic," Brock said as he reached to tear out another page.

"Stop it!" I pursed my lips. "Was my sketchbook open when you stole my brownie?" I slowly turned my head left and right to indicate no. "Or when you had to go to the bathroom suddenly today?"

"Still!" Brock looked confused, but that had never stopped him before.

"It's all in your head, you stupid bully," I said with a snarl. "Tell the truth for once. You're making all of this up."

The playground remained frozen in silence as we faced off. I advanced, holding the pencil like a weapon in my hand. Brock backed up. Jenna stood ready to break it up.

"Brock Sullivan, put down my book this instant!" I yelled as I pushed my face forward and my arms straight back.

"What is going on here?" Ms. Quinn marched quickly over to where the two of us were squaring off. "Well?"

I stopped glaring at Brock to look at the principal. I stepped back and felt my heart pounding in my ears. I inhaled slowly. Behind Ms. Quinn, I could see the whole school watching.

"Tell her, Brock," I said, my mouth tight, as I exhaled slowly through pursed lips. With the pencil, I drew a little doodle in the air.

"I.. She… It's…" Brock tried to blame me, but he just couldn't say the words.

He shook his head, then set down my sketchbook.

"I uh… I took her sketchbook and was going to tear it up, Ms. Quinn," he said and looked around like he was searching for an escape. "I tease her all the time, and I thought she was using magic to get back at me." He slapped his hand over his mouth.

"A rare bit of truth from Mr. Brock Sullivan," said Ms. Quinn. "Well, if Miss Shannongale was using magic, the fact that you are telling the truth might be the first real evidence of it."

The playground erupted in laughter that was probably more relief than anything.

"It's… argh!" Brock shouted as he seemed to wrestle with his mouth. "She wasn't doing anything. I picked on her. She never does anything." He hung his head and shook it.

"Well, Mr. Sullivan, that's very honest of you," Ms. Quinn said. "And even though you told the truth for the first time in years, I will still want to talk to you in my office. Go sit there now, and do not disturb Mrs. O'Shea."

"Yes, ma'am," he huffed as he trundled off to the principal's office. The kids scattered across the playground now that we diffused the bomb.

Ms. Quinn turned, handed me the sketchbook, and smiled. I bent and picked up the drawing Brock had torn out of my book.

"Jenna, I would like a word with Miss Shannongale," Ms. Quinn said.

"Yes, ma'am," replied Jenna. She saw one of the older boys standing with one foot on a ball, so she kicked it out from under him and raced toward the field with four boys chasing her.

The principal waited until everybody was out of earshot, then she put her hand on my shoulder.

"Well, this worked out rather nicely," Ms. Quinn whispered with a wink. "Better than I could have hoped."

"What do you mean?" I cocked my head to the side. "What worked out?"

"An educated guess says you enchanted Brock Sullivan to tell the truth," smiled Ms. Quinn. "To be honest, I couldn't have asked for a better ending."

The principal looked up to the roof, and I followed her gaze. There sat Tom Sceal wearing a big grin that seemed to reach from one pointy ear to the other.

"Come on, Tom," said Ms. Quinn. "You've earned yourself a holiday."

"You knew?" I stammered.

"Of course, dear," said Ms. Quinn. "Who do you think binds and unbinds him?"

"Wait, you're a…" I started but didn't know how to finish.

"Centuries ago, they might have called me a witch, dear," Ms. Quinn said with a wink. "But I prefer the term, *Sorceress*. It's much more powerful, don't you think?"

CHAPTER TWENTY-TWO

Mistakes Were Made

"Ms. Quinn is the one who binds and unbinds Tom Sceal," my mom nodded. "You were so depressed, I thought maybe if he unlocked your drawing, school would be better."

"You knew?" I asked.

"I didn't want him to unlock your magic, though," mom said. "That was dangerous."

"Mom!" I couldn't believe my ears. "You knew?" She looked at me and started laughing. She swooped me up in her arms and hugged me.

"I did, Ash," mom replied. "And I'm happy that it's over."

"Mom, I um…" I started as we sat down at the table. "I don't think it's all the way over."

"What do you mean?" said mom, searching my eyes.

"I tried to undo Tom Sceal's magic," I said.

"You did?" Mom looked around, then smiled as Coven jumped up on my lap and started purring.

"Yes, but it kind of backfired," I continued. "And now I don't have to blow on things to make them real." I looked down and petted my sweet, black kitten.

"Oh dear, you mean there's no control?" Mom sat down across from me.

"I have to be the control, mom," I replied. "Like you always said, I have to learn to control my temper."

"And can you?" said mom.

"When Brock took my sketchbook and threatened to tear it apart, I felt my eyes go golden," I explained as I stroked the kitten's soft fur. "A pencil even flew into my hands. But I knew that if I got my usual level of mad, it would only make things worse. And I remembered how I hated the way I felt yesterday when I thought I might have killed him."

I bowed my head and kissed Coven on the ear. The kitten looked up and mewed. I looked at my mom, but my tears were making it hard to see. "I decided to focus on turning Brock's lies into telling the truth."

"Did that work?" Mom asked. I nodded.

"He confessed everything to Ms. Quinn. She was quite impressed," I smiled a bit. "He hated it, but he couldn't stop telling the truth."

"Well, I hope that enchantment lasts," said mom with a smile. "And how is Jenna with all this?"

"I think she kind of loves having a magical friend," I said with a giggle. "I made her a muffin for a snack and then enchanted her feet so she could play even better."

"And did that work?" Mom asked.

"She said she felt like Lionel Messi, Cristiano Ronaldo, Megan Rapinoe, and Alex Morgan all rolled together in one."

"I have no idea what you just said, but I take it that was a success," said mom.

"She was dribbling circles around the boys on the playground," I said. "I went to watch her. She's amazing."

"And your report?" said mom.

"We finished it this afternoon," smiled Aisling. "We even included Brock's story about me turning him into a frog and made it sound like half of the things people said to convict witches in Salem. So now nobody believes him."

"I'm so glad you found a friend and your place at that school," said mom. "Now, what should we make for dinner?"

"Well, I was thinking…" I said as the doorbell rang.

My mom shot me a look and laughed.

"I hope you don't mind, mom," I said sheepishly. "But I kinda traded the kale in our fridge for it."

"You what?" Mom looked shocked.

"Tom Sceal taught me that magic is an exchange," I said. "With Brock, I traded his lies for the truth. Then I traded my anger at him to help Jenna do what she loved. And for dinner..."

"You traded our healthy kale for..." Mom said with a chuckle as she went to the door. She returned with a large pizza box. "I guess I'll allow it tonight," she said, smiling. "Let's watch a movie. I know it's been an intense week."

"Totally!" I grabbed our lemonades and plopped down on the couch. Coven ran over, jumped up, and joined us.

~

As the light crept into the room the next morning, I smiled. For the first time in an exceptionally long time, I was not dreading school. I got up and washed my face, slipped back into my room, and pulled out my favorite jeans and black-and-white striped shirt. I pulled on my red, high-top gym shoes. Coven stirred, looked at me like I was out of my mind, stretched, and went back to sleep. It made me smile.

"See you after school, sleepyhead," I whispered as I rubbed my kitten's head. I quietly opened my door and saw mom sitting on the couch, sipping her coffee and leafing through a book.

"Good morning, sweetheart," she smiled. "Where are you off to?"

"School," I said. I looked at my mom lounging, then back at my room, confused.

"You'll wait a long time for the bus," she said. "It's Saturday."

"What?" My eye roll was so spectacular it involved my whole head. Jenna would have been impressed. "Are you kidding me?" I groaned.

"Come and sit with me," mom said. "I want to show you something."

I dropped down onto the couch and curled up next to my mom. I kicked off my shoes and pulled my legs up.

"I love these patterns," mom said to me as she shared a book of drawings.

"That looks like a braid," I said.

"Yes," replied mom, with a smile. "In the old country, these images represented loyalty, faith, and family. They have no start and no end."

"They're infinite?" I asked.

"Yes, and they're also protection against evil spirits," said mom. "Which we might need now."

"Why?" I looked up at my mom, whose forehead was wrinkled in concern.

"Well, Ash, I know you want to be normal, but that's never going to happen," said mom with a resigned smile. "You are incredibly magical now."

"Yeah, I guess that's one more thing to make me a bit different," I scrunched up the left side of my mouth and nodded.

"And magical people are magnets for troublesome folks," mom said as she leaned down and kissed my head.

"Like Tom Sceal?" I asked. "Or more like Brock Sullivan and Tiffany Treacle?"

"All of them and more," said mom. "So, I thought we would spend this morning drawing some shield knots like this one."

"The Celtic shield knot looks like a square within a circle," I read aloud from the book. "It was used on battle shields and placed on sick people to ward off evil spirits and other danger."

"Sounds like exactly what we need," mom said.

"I'd like a shield," I agreed.

The doorbell rang. I looked at mom, who smiled at me. She went to the door and opened it. She returned with a small box.

"What is it?" I asked.

"I ordered these when you told me about Tom Sceal," she said. "I guess they got here a day too late to help with him." She pulled out two forest green boxes and handed one to me. Inside was a Celtic shield knot etched into a hammered silver pendant on a silver chain.

"You must be careful with this," mom said as she reached around and put it around my neck. *"An cailín seo a chosaint agus í a choinneáil slán,"* she said under her breath. Then she moved her hands together, up, and away. The necklace sparkled.

"It's warm," I said.

"I just enchanted it," said mom with a gentle smile.

"Can I enchant yours?" I asked. Mom smiled and nodded. I whispered, "Protect this lass and keep her safe." Then I closed my eyes, took a deep breath, and traced the knot with my finger on the pendant. When I opened my eyes, the necklace shimmered.

"How did you know that was what I said?" Mom asked, studying me. "I spoke in…"

"Gaelic," I replied. "Tom Sceal said it was one of the skills I acquired when my spell backfired."

Mom pulled me close and kissed my head. Not to be left out, Coven jumped up on the back of the couch and climbed down between us. He squirmed into a small space on my lap and began purring. I giggled and brushed his muzzle with the back of my finger.

Mom smiled at both of us. "I'm not sure who needs more protection magic. Us or the world."

Made in the USA
Las Vegas, NV
24 January 2024

84593049R10094